About the Author

Ted Curtis is an up and coming writer working in all fields, but not advertising. He is currently developing a radio play on the jam, the miners strike and the IRA, as well as a collection of short stories about Swindon in the eighties. Random samples of new work can be found at http://antsy-pantsy.blogspot.com/ During the 1990s he had some success in the small press, and even with Serpents Tail, but he decided to concentrate on his drinking instead. He was very good at it too. Now he's back.

He can be contacted at ted.curtis@aktivix.org

the darkening light

Ted Curtis

For Cruz,
big love missus,
mad Teddy xxx.

Itchy Monkey Press

Itchy Monkey Press

Copyright 2014 Ted Curtis

Published by Itchy Monkey Press

Itchy Monkey Press -
http://www.talesfromthepunkside.com/

Cover design by Jon Leftley

Printed in the UK by Imprint Digital

ISBN: 978-1-291-74626-6

Acknowledgements

With special thanks for assistance with the text to Timea Kegli, Nigel Cotterill, Mike Dines, Robert Dellar, Jon Active and Felicity Stephen.

Note

This is presented as a work of fiction. That means that while you may recognise some bands and their lyrics, and even the names of some people, none of this happened. It's fiction.

the darkening light

It is a Saturday morning, early, it is April 1st 1986 and you are hungover to hell. You have recently discovered how to make homebrewed lager but you are not very good at it. You are not very good at drinking either, but neither is anybody else that you know, and so you have no reference point. You are an anarchist punk. You have been an anarchist punk for about three years, and in that short time – really, since the time that you saw crass on their last ever tour – the anarchist punk scene seems to have gone all to hell. Where once there were an infinite variety of identikit cardboard cutout vegan black clad revolutionaries, everyone either in a band or making a fanzine or both, now there is the infusion and the corrosive influence of metal. Metal is eating anarchist punk from the inside out, shitting everywhere and on everyone as it goes, poisoning everything that it touches. You are in Swindon, once a small market town, then the hub of the national rail system, but by the time that you get there the railway works has gone, shut down in an orgy of monetarist restructuring, and it is now the fastest growing industrial town in western Europe. Companies have moved here from London, attracted by favourable business rates and other sweeteners, and it is becoming a mecca for both the yuppies and for transient workers from Scotland and the north of England, desperate for temporary employment, their own communities decimated and laid waste by that same monetarist restructuring. You do not want to work. This is why you need to make homebrew. You are waiting for the vegan revolution. You are waiting for anarchy. You have moved here from the most beautiful city on earth, you think for love, or perhaps because there are more anarchist vegans here than in your home town, but really you are just running.

You take a hefty swig from an unlabeled two litre plastic bottle of homebrewed lager to propel you into the day. The sediment moves around in the bottle mercilessly, the scum swimming to the top, and, catching the stench of rotting yeast through your nostrils, you swallow a dry heave. You cough, you take another pull at the bottle, you put the bottle down. You put your face into your hands, knead at your eye sockets, you pick up the bottle, you take another pull at the bottle and you begin to come alive. You screw the cap back onto the bottle, pick up your glasses, squint at the lenses. You used to say to Green Hat Eddie that you could gauge how good a time you had had the night before by seeing how misted up and dirtied the lenses of your glasses are in the morning. By all accounts it must have been a pretty good night, the lenses are filthy and one of the arms is bent right back, but you can remember only small sections of the night before, and soon they will be gone too. There is a yelling from the bottom of the stairs, *come on Frank, get your fucking shit together, it's past ten o'clock. Come on you drunken fucker.* It is Sarah, the love that you thought you had moved here for, one of the anarchist vegans. There is no need for you to dress because you have slept in your clothes. You get out from under the single filthy blanket, pull on your wellies, and you try to arrange your glasses about your head after first wiping the lenses on your dirty black T-shirt. The T-shirt is *metallica, master of puppets,* the sleeves roughly removed with a pair of jagged edged scissors, the kind used for cutting out the tags for Christmas presents from old cards from the year before. You shoplifted them from Superdrug. You don't really like metallica, they are metal, but it was a cheap black T-shirt, one from a job lot that fell off the back of a lorry. You stand, look around for carrier bags, you find some and then you put four two litre bottles of the homebrew into them and you check for your keys, leave your room and go downstairs. You are all going to a squat gig in Wood Green, north London.

There is nobody downstairs but the front door is open, and so you go out onto the street, pulling the door shut behind you. Across the street next to the new community centre a group of people who dress just like you in the *metallica* T-shirts that fell off the back of a lorry are standing around a battered old Leyland Sherpa van, bought for £120 from the proceeds of anarchist punk benefit gigs for the hunt saboteurs, smoking roll ups. They are waiting for you, you have been making them late. They are, in no particular order, Steve and Sarah who live in the house with you, number 13 church street; Mark Dooley; Pete & Mary; Hop; Neil; Gogs; Graham. Only Gogs has a silly punk name. You can remember when almost everybody you knew had a silly punk name. Not Stan Bastardly or anything stagey like that, just names that had no relation to anyone's given names. It was a break from the past, the end of history. Now Hop is only called Hop not because he dances the pogo very badly, which he does, but because his given name is Hopkins. Green Hat Eddie might have come but Green Hat Eddie is dead from methadone. Opiates were once frowned upon by your subgroup but even that is falling by the wayside now. You mutter helloes at one another and you all pile into the back of the van. Steve is the driver, and Mary gets to sit up front with him. Mary is something of a princess. You think that this is a class thing. She is from Shrivenham. Shrivenham has its own beagle hunt.

You leave Gorse Hill and head out through Ferndale and toward the M4. There is nothing happening in Gorse Hill. There never is. On Wednesday afternoons the shops are all shut for a half day, it's like Wootton Bassett without the funerals. Soon you are past the new industrial estates, Readers Digest, Thorn EMI, metal box, and onto the motorway. Metal box used to make you laugh, you thought that it was an industrial estate that had been named after a punk rock album, but you found out that it was only the name of a company that manufactures paint tins. Now things are making you laugh less and less all the time.

Packages of roll ups are passed around and the chatter begins. The content of the chatter is not even worth mentioning. After the nicotine has woken you up a little bit, you pull out a bottle of homebrewed lager and you take three or four pulls in rapid succession, swallowing hard. You offer it around but there are few takers, they have all either heard about your homebrew or they have experienced it directly, briefly. Some of the others pull out tins of red stripe and breaker lager from their own carrier bags, one or two bottles of cider. You think about asking for some cider to mix with your homebrew and make snakebites but you know that you will be refused so you stick with what you know. The stench of your rotten yeasty brew fills the van and, turning his head, Steve calls out melodramatically from the drivers seat, oh for fucks sake Frank, not the *homebrew*, and he turns around and grins at you. Everybody laughs. Steve is a popular man, he saw *crass* many times, he knows *chumbawamba* and he is the one of only two people among you who knows how to drive. Mary admonishes him and tells him to watch the road.

Some time passes amid the chatter and then you are at Membury services and Steve announces that this will be your only stop before London, that you had better get any crisps and anything else that you want and make use of the facilities while you can. He adds that he doesn't think there will be much in the way of facilities at the squat gig. Nobody but Steve is sure which part of London you are going to and Hop asks him where it is, this squat, and he tells everybody as he is carefully reversing into a parking space that it is an old dole office in Wood Green, which is in north London. You have never heard of Wood Green, this is many years before the ricin plot. Hop asks Steve whether Wood Green is anywhere near the Clarendon hotel and Steve tells him that no, that's in Hammersmith, Hammersmith is in west London and the Clarendon hotel was never a squat anyway. As he finishes parking and turns the engine off he turns around, and he asks everyone if they would prefer that he find a car park in west London so that you can get onto the tube, or if he should try to find parking closer to the Wood Green dole house. The response is unanimous. Nobody wants the added expense of tube fares, which have gone through the roof since the demise of the GLC, and there is some chatter about the confusion of the tube system with all its different coloured lines. Gogs, who has spent some time in east London with the angry art house punk band *the apostles*, begins explaining where the different coloured tube lines go to, north south east west, the major connective hubs, and how it's really quite simple once you get used to it, but the back doors of the van have opened and everybody is piling out toward the main concourse of the service station. Nobody is interested in coloured tube lines and the four cardinal directions, everybody needs to piss, and anyway there is also the matter that later, somebody will inevitably get lost down there, you are certain to get split up and London is a very big place. It's fourteen miles across and nine miles deep you think that you once read somewhere, and you have no idea at what time the different coloured tube lines stop working for the night, or when they start up again in the morning, especially a Sunday morning, or at what time the squat gig might finish. So you pile out after them, still clutching your second bottle of homebrewed lager, and you follow them towards the main concourse of the motorway service station as you hear Steve calling after you, *fifteen minutes, fifteen minutes and I'm gone, fifteen minutes and I'm leaving you all behind!*

While everybody else is in the toilets, and having carefully screwed the cap onto your bottle in order to mask the stench of the rotting yeast, you saunter into the inevitable branch of WH Smith and you deftly squeeze between the other customers in the newspapers and magazines section to catch a crafty glimpse of the covers of the soft porn magazines on the top shelf, remembering to check over first your left shoulder, then your right, every two to three seconds in case you are seen. You look down at the headlines of the newspapers to provide yourself with a cover story in case this does happen. You are busy constructing fervent opinions in your head so that your cover story will be credible. Over Athens a TWA jet has been bombed and four people, including an eight-month old baby, have been sucked out of a hole in the side. The American military submarine the Nathaniel Green has run aground in the Irish sea. World oil prices have dipped below $10 a barrel. You know that this is against the rules, the gawking at the soft porn, but you are very lonely. You had thought that punk rock and anarchist politics, that veganism and a proper *relationship*, that these things would alleviate your loneliness, but thus far you have been proved wrong. It is still there, burning in every muscle and fibre of your being. You stare at the magazine covers for some time, moving around occasionally. The service station is busy, people are on their way to football matches and holidays. You used to like football but your interest waned, and a love of football has not yet become *de rigeur* in anarchist punk circles. Finally, after some very tasty comments and ripe stares from holidaymakers and bescarfed football supporters, you sense that you have outstayed your welcome and you walk out of the WH Smith and toward the toilets. The toilets are by the entrance and when you get there you see that there is a queue for the gents stretching all of the way outside the building. You decide that you cannot wait, you are full to bursting, you are full to bursting with the homebrewed lager and the loneliness, and you decide that as it is so busy nobody will notice if you nip around the corner from the entrance and onto a grass verge and relieve yourself there. You put your bottle onto the ground and you are halfway through your piss when a sales assistant from WH Smith, returning from a cigarette break and recognising you from earlier, from the newspapers and magazines and the soft porn section, comes running over yelling. *You filthy dirty punk bastard* he screams at you, and just as you look around he charges you and pushes you to the ground. Piss goes all of the way down your thighs and some of it even gets onto him, and he becomes apoplectic with disgust and rage. There is a commotion now, people are gathering around and cursing. You stand and you stagger back toward the car park and the van, seeing that everybody else is standing around it, smoking roll ups, waiting for you, as earlier. You must have got lost in time staring at the magazine covers and memorising the newspaper headlines. You hear the sales assistant calling out that he is calling the police as he goes back inside the concourse, and you tell Steve, who has been conscientiously topping up the radiator of the van's engine with water from your discarded homebrewed lager bottle, that you had best get going now. A couple of your friends mutter something sarcastic and you all pile back into the van, and before you know it you are back onto the M4 and heading east.

After about ten minutes Mark Dooley pulls a half bottle of Teachers whisky from his man bag, and he takes a hefty swig, says something about it hitting the spot like nothing else on this earth, belches exaggeratedly, and passes it around. When it reaches you, you take more than your fair share and you begin to go into blackout. You have had alcoholic blackouts before, you have had then almost from the start of your drinking when Richard Whiteman told that all you need for a good night out is a fiver for ten fags and four cans of Special Brew, but your more recent blackouts have been very strange. They have been more like a kind of disembodied, dissociative lucid dreaming. Earlier in the year at the Mermaid, an enormous wino pub in Birmingham where they held all day punk gigs every weekend for many months, this was when the lucid dreaming almost blackouts began. You would drink on the way up there in the back of a different van and then you would find that upstairs at the Mermaid, upstairs at the Mermaid where the gigs were held, they were selling strong scrumpy cider at the bar for sixty pence a pint. Downstairs at the Mermaid, downstairs at the Mermaid where you had to walk through the bar to get to the stairs and up into the gig, was like a deleted scene from the film *Mad Max*; even more so than at the average crusty anarchist punk squat gig, which is saying something. This was the first time that you had ever seen winos drinking who were not on the street. You had always assumed that such people would be instantly barred from all proper drinking establishments and you realized that, crusty anarchist punk squat gigs notwithstanding, you had led a pretty sheltered existence up until now, but that this is probably soon to change. You realise that there are some very rough pubs out there and that they will feature in your soon to be present if you carry on the road that you have been travelling for the past two or three years. Upstairs at the Mermaid, you would nip into the main hall periodically to check out the bands that you liked, and then duck back into the bar for more and more of the cheap scrumpy cider. By the time that that the gig is over and it is time to drive back down to Wiltshire, at one or two in the morning, you are in full lucid dreaming blackout mode. Full lucid dreaming blackout mode goes something like this: you are aware of your surroundings, on and off, you can barely speak but you can stand although you largely do not want to stand, but you are convinced that nothing is real. That you are in a dream. You are constantly asking Sarah whether this is all real, *is this a dream Sarah* you ask her over and over, and she tells you in a very pissed off tone that *yes Frank, this is real, this isn't a dream Frank*, but you are unable to believe her. One time you hoik down your jeans and your pants and you go to take a dump in one corner of the van, and you have to be manhandled back into your clothes before you can properly let go, but your rescuers get piss all over their hands and they are very annoyed with you. Another time you all emerge from the gig to find that the van has a flat tyre and it has to be jacked up so that the wheel can be changed, and you want to sleep and so you climb into the back of the van and you refuse to move because you believe that this is all a dream, that none of this is real.

But for now you are not in lucid dreaming mode, you are in simple blackout. You simply have no recollection of the journey from the time that you neck more than your fair share of the whisky, until the time you arrive at the squat gig in Wood green. Wood Green dole house is just around the corner from Wood Green tube station and parking has been found nearby. When you come out of blackout you are standing next to Mark Dooley on the stairs. Mark Dooley who is trying to talk to Monti and Alien from the Hackney Hell Crew. They are both members of *the sons of badbreath*, who are both playing later. There is a can of Special Brew, mostly gone, in your hand. Sarah is standing next to you trying to hold your other hand, and you are both listening in on the conversation, which seems to be quite one sided. Mark Dooley keeps asking Monti how he is and what he has been up to lately, but Monti doesn't seem to know who Mark Dooley is and

Alien is standing to the side of him, drinking and occasionally giggling but saying nothing. Eventually Monti ask Mark Dooley his name and where he is from, and tells him that he has not been up to much lately, just squatting and sniffing glue and drinking Special Brew and doing Hackney Hell crew stuff. Mark Dooley asks him what time *the sons of badbreath* are playing and Monti says that he doesn't know, that it's chaos up there and that's just the way he likes it. Alien whispers something into Monti's ear and they make their excuses and go on up the stairs to where the bands are playing. You all follow close behind them, you follow the noise, and Mark Dooley keeps turning around to you and saying, that was Monti, that was Monti from the Hackney hell Crew, that was my mate Monti.

When you get into the hall Mark Dooley pulls out a half bottle of vodka from his man bag and he disappears into the throng, which is quite sizeable for a Saturday afternoon. *atavistic* from Kent are playing, they are halfway through their short set. They are fast and furious and they somehow do not look quite punk. They look like determinedly academic sixth formers on a mission, they wear all black and their hair is short but not too short, not dyed, they wear black T-shirts with black v-neck jumpers over the top, black jeans and black trainers. You met them the year before when they played at a disastrous all-dayer on a council estate in Swindon. There was skateboard-related violence and all of the windows got smashed, there was rather a lot of blood and the police were called. You stand and watch the rest of their set, finish your Special Brew, and after they have finished you and Sarah both go up to say hello, and they are quite friendly but they are packing up their gear, they want to get back to Kent in time for *the two ronnies,* and Patrick works in a nursing home and he is working a twelve hour night shift starting at 6pm.

Next up are *antisect*, who are partway through their change from fast punk noise to deep and edgy metallic soundscapes. They have been through all manner of line up changes in the previous year, but just for today Caroline is back and they are doing a lot of their old stuff, the stuff from before their album was recorded. They do *four minutes past midnight* and then they read out a list of all the wars that have taken place since the end of World War II while Pete Lyons makes high pitched screeching noises on his guitar, and occasionally screams *peace?* into his microphone. Then they launch into *welcome to the new dark ages* and everybody begins dancing. When the song is over they do another old one, *what the fuck are you doing here?* which is more screeching guitar noises with Caroline and Tim yelling the question over the top amid chaotic drumming, and then they go back into the music, alternating between new and old stuff, and they play for another twenty minutes or so. You stand, enraptured, thinking that this beautiful noise is what life is really all about, what this whole thing is really all about, this thing that you left your life in the most beautiful city in the world behind for. When they finish you are just thinking that you badly need a piss and another drink, and you turn to Sarah to ask her where the van is parked and where is Steve with the keys so that you can get at the remainder of your homebrewed lager. You are just about to ask her this when there is a commotion from the far side of the hall and you look across and you see that there are people running away from it. When enough people have peeled away from the commotion you see Pete and Mary facing you, and Pete calls out to you, *Frank, Frank, it's Mark, I think he's hurt*, and you run across and you see that it is indeed Mark Dooley, he is laying on the floor face down and not moving. Against your better judgement you kneel down beside him and you roll him over onto his back, muttering something about some first aid training that you received the previous year while you were working part time in the most beautiful city in the world on a youth training scheme, none of which you can remember now, but you have seen various television dramas and you know that this is what people do. You had assumed that he had been punched out, but as you are rolling him over he begins to gurgle and mumble, and you see that his face is unmarked. You try to remember your first aid training from the previous year, but all that you can recall are some exercises with a dummy swathed in bandages sitting in a chair, and something about mouth-to-mouth resuscitation. None of the exercises seem to be relevant as Mark Dooley is not swathed in bandages and sitting in a chair, and you do not much fancy the prospect of giving him mouth to mouth resuscitation and besides, he is mumbling and gurgling and thus he is obviously still breathing. You turn around to ask Pete and Mary what has happened to him, but Mary has run off somewhere and Pete has turned a deathly shade of pale, even in the darkness and the gloom of the squatted Wood Green dole house upstairs hall, you can clearly see that he has turned a deathly shade of pale. You remember that Pete has some kind of a pathological aversion to the sight of blood and you see that he is pointing down at one of Mark Dooley's arms and stammering something. You look down at Mark Dooley's arm and you see that the wrist is quite shredded, his bootlace bracelets intermingled with loose flesh and gore. You look back up at Pete and you tell him to take a deep breath and to hold it in and count backwards down from ten to one, to exhale slowly through his nose, to repeat the process and then to try to tell you what has happened. He does this and then he is able to speak a little more clearly and it turns out that Mark Dooley has had an argument with Colin Jerwood from the often controversial animal rights band *conflict*. Colin Jerwood is well over six feet tall and Mark Dooley is not a tall person, he is maybe 5'8", and Mark Dooley is often getting drunk and picking fights on the slightest of pretexts with very tall people. Steve has remarked on this before, he has read something about it and refers to it as *the Napoleon complex*. Mark Dooley has picked a random argument with Colin Jerwood, and while Colin Jerwood has been standing there in his overcoat listening to his tirade, Mark Dooley has taken a random swing at him. Colin Jerwood has stepped deftly to one side and Mark Dooley's momentum has carried him forward a foot or two and partway through an already broken frosted glass window, shredding his wrist. He has pulled himself out of its jagged spikes, further damaging his arm, and then he has reeled around for a few moments before collapsing onto his front. It is a minor miracle that he did not damage his face as he fell, momentarily unconscious, but now he is coming round again, gurgling and mumbling. You and Pete manage to get him onto his feet, and you walk him through the sea of parting onlookers and you get him down the stairs and outside, looking for a telephone box, an ambulance and medical assistance. As you leave the hall *axegrinder* are tuning up amid the chaos.

Together with Pete you walk Mark Dooley slowly up onto Lordship Lane and you locate a telephone box. You sit Mark Dooley on the pavement, you prop him up against a wall and you call for an ambulance and tell the operator what has happened. While you wait for the ambulance Saturday shoppers are walking around you into the road, they are parting around you like the sea of onlookers from inside the Wood Green dole house. Pete has removed his T-shirt and given it to you, and you have tied it tightly around Mark Dooley's damaged wrist to form a crude punk rock tourniquet, and now Pete is now stripped to the waist. The ambulance takes some time to arrive, it is a busy Saturday afternoon in almost central London. There is nothing for you to do but sit and wait, periodically checking on Mark Dooley to see that he is still conscious. Mark Dooley continues to mutter and to gurgle.

You had heard of Mark Dooley before you ever met him, his reputation preceded him. While you were still living in the most beautiful city in the world but travelling regularly to Swindon for small anarchist punk gigs, you heard the stories of his drunken escapades, often involving fights with tall people whom he did not know. One time he tried to take on a small team of football casuals from Luton outside the railway station but they had given him a couple of slaps, pushed him over, and then gone on inside to catch their train, laughing. Another time he had produced a butterfly knife in the Castle hotel on North Street, trying to twirl it like a baton through his fingers before dropping it several times, calling out *who wants it then who wants it then* over and over, and then attracting the attention of the bar staff, who banned him for a week. When you did finally meet him it was in a squat in the most beautiful city in the world off the Lower Bristol Road, the first place that you lived in briefly after fleeing the home of your parents. You had dropped acid for the first time after watching *the mob* and *disturbance from fear*, Steve's band, at the *ring o bells* in Widcombe. You were tripping hard and seeing purple snow and he took the piss out of you relentlessly, saying things like *ooh look at that cosmic man I'm tripping my nuts off man*, every time that you opened your mouth. Later on in the summer, the summer after the Wood Green dole house, he will turn up at your door looking for Steve. He has walked from the other side of town in the blistering summer heat but Steve is not in, he has hitch hiked to a gig in Leamington Spa to see a girlfriend, and when you tell Mark Dooley this and you ask him in for a cup of tea, he has said *no, it's alright Frank*, and he has turned on his heel and walked off down the road, and this the first time that you realise that you do not have a single friend in Swindon, that you never did have.

When the ambulance arrives it pulls up onto the pavement and a nurse and the ambulance driver get out, it is before the days of paramedics. You and Pete jump up and Mark Dooley jumps up too, but he immediately collapses back down again. The nurse comes over and she crouches over Mark Dooley and she starts to ask him what he has done to himself, she holds up three fingers to ask him to count them, and he immediately makes a grab for her tits with his bloodied arm, and she slaps him twice around the face hard, first this way and then that, and he falls back and he starts to cry. After a minute he calms down a little, hawks up some snot and expels it to the side, and the nurse manages to get a proper look at his damaged wrist. It is cut open pretty badly and you lean in for a closer look, you can see veins and tendons, exposed and visceral, and you are suddenly overcome with nausea and you back away. The nurse says to you *that's it mate, stand back and let me do my job*, and you look around for Pete and you see that he has gotten a closer look at Mark Dooley's wrist as well because he has staggered over to the wall and is throwing up against it. Shaking now, you stagger over to him and you put the palm of your hand onto his back to comfort him and you begin massaging his neck, and then he turns around, he has finished puking now, and he says something to you. The stench of puke on his breath is really quite overpowering in the cool spring air, and you begin to nauseate again. You lean into him and he grabs you, and you both sit down together on the pavement, falling into a heap. The Saturday shoppers continue to move around you into the road, flowing freely on their way, not really giving you a second glance, and you both take a few minutes to collect yourselves. Pete says something about *antisect* being very good, that he's never seen them play live before, and then he says something about smelling salts and he reaches into his pocket and produces a bottle of amyl nitrate. He unscrews the cap and takes a huff on it, then he passes it to you and you take a generous couple of inhalations, one good long one in each nostril and you are propelled back into the day, and just as you hand the bottle back to him the nurse calls you over and you stand in unison and you go back over to the nurse and to Mark Dooley. Without thinking, Pete passes the bottle of amyl nitrate to the nurse and she takes it and she takes a couple of generous inhalations from it too, and then she throws her head back and she cackles wildly. The ambulance driver is standing over you with his arms folded and she passes the bottle to him, and he takes it and he has a couple of goes on it too, before passing it back to Pete and folding his arms across his chest again. Pete puts the cap back on the bottle and he puts it back into his jeans pocket. You look up at him, slightly amazed that on-duty NHS staff could be such flagrant drug abusers, and he shrugs his shoulders and you remember that amyl nitrate is quite legal, just like alcohol.

The nurse has given Mark Dooley a shot of something in his arm and she is rubbing neat alcohol into the puncture wound to clean it, and she turns to you and asks you where you are from, whether you are local, she asks you whether you live in Harringey. You have never heard of

Harringey, you think that it might be a nearby military aircraft hangar, when you are hitch hiking around the country to small anarchist punk gigs you are forever getting lifts from people who think that you must be in the military because you dress all in black or in army fatigues. You tell her that no, you are not local, you are all from Wiltshire, you are up here for the day for a squat gig in the old dole house round the corner, you tell her that it's possible that *heresy* are playing later. In your bemused state, and having seen her having a go on Pete's amyl nitrate, you think that she might be interested in the squat gig, thinking of some young women you used to know who worked in the unemployment benefit office in Aberystwyth and who used to turn up in the evenings to a squat on Marine Terrace and chase the dragon with you through the night. The nurse pulls a pair of scissors from her medical bag, putting the disposable syringe that she administered the shot to Mark Dooley with away, and she produces a small pair of scissors and she goes to cut away the bootlace bangles from Mark Dooley's wrist so that she can properly get at the wound and treat it and he punches her in the face, it's not much of a blow but it snaps her neck back, she isn't expecting it, and she instinctively sticks the head on him. Mark Dooley begins to cry again and she leans into the side of his head and she whispers menacingly into his right ear, *I'm sorry mate, I had to do that.*

The nurse cuts away Mark Dooley's bootlace bangles and places them carefully into her medical bag, and then she produces more rubbing alcohol and she cleans the wound, gently and carefully she cleans the wound, and then she gets a bandage and some sticking tape and a safety pin and she wraps the wound up too, and she secures the wound, and you are quite surprised to notice that there is no blood seeping through, it is an expert job. She stands and she turns to face you and Pete, Pete who has turned a shade of deathly pale again, and she tells you that Mark Dooley really needs to get some stitches in that wound, that he really needs to get to a hospital, they can take you to the Whittington if you like but they really can't force you to go, and anyway they have another call. You thank her but Pete is saying nothing, he is swallowing hard, you thank her and you tell her that you think you will be alright now and you go to shake her hand, and after a pause she takes your hand and she shakes it briefly. She looks at you strangely and tells you that you should get Mark Dooley to a hospital as soon as you get back to Wiltshire, that *that wound needs further treatment*, and then the ambulance driver and the nurse are getting back into their ambulance and then they are gone, and you stand there in silence for a moment and you wonder whether any of this has been real.

On the way back to the gig you stop off at an off license and you get more Special Brew and

Mark Dooley gets a half bottle of vodka and ten cigarettes and you tell him to be careful, *careful Mark mate* you say to him, and he says something dismissive and cynical back to you, but you can't work out exactly what the words are because of the drink and the drugs in him and the drink and the drugs in you. You get back to the gig just as Steve is coming out with the van keys, he is beaming wildly and he says something about some speed but then he sees Mark Dooley and his face drops. He asks you what has happened and you tell him at length, Pete is still not speaking, and then he says *cosmic* and he walks with you to the van while Mark Dooley and Pete go back into the gig. Steve opens the van and you jump into the back, and you rummage through the mess of empty carrier bags and beer cans and half size vodka and whisky bottles, and you eventually find the last of your carrier bags with only one bottle of your homebrewed lager inside. You feel as if the experience around the corner with the ambulance crew and the Saturday shoppers and the rescue of Mark Dooley has sobered you up a little, the amyl nitrate notwithstanding, and so you uncap the bottle and you take a hefty whack on it and it is only as you hold the bottle up to the light that you realize that it is almost half gone, and that what is left is swimming in sediment and rotting yeast, the smell of it making you gag again. You swallow down a pukey belch and get out of the back of the van, and Steve is leaning against it making a roll-up and he asks you if you have finished and you tell him that you have, and he secures it and together you go back inside the Wood Green dole house and up the stairs.

When you get back into the gig you find that you have just missed *the sons of badbreath* and that *eat shit* are tuning up, if that is what it can be called, and then they launch into their opening number, *fuck living*. You begin dancing with the heaving mass of sweaty and disconnected bodies, each of them believing that they are special, and you finish as much of your rotten yeasty homebrewed lager as you can manage, and then you throw the bottle over your shoulder and into the mass of the crowd. It showers everyone briefly with foam and rotten yeast but mostly they seem not to notice, *eat shit* do not miss a beat, and as you turn around you see that it has gone all over somebody called Pus. You do not know Pus but you have met him on occasion, he is another member of the Hackney Hell Crew, he used to roadie for *antisect* and he has a prison tattoo across his left cheek, just under the eye socket, a prison tattoo that says *goat-breath*. The previous year you had shared a dining table with him at Membury services, *antisect* and *dirt* were giving you a lift back to the most beautiful city in the world after a gig in Bristol, they were driving back to London, and Pus had been scouring the other dining tables in the almost deserted service station, looking for leftover food. He had finally come back to your dining table where you were drinking vegan black tea, carrying a plate half filled with cold baked beans and half eaten sausages congealed in hardening grease, you had looked at him strangely and he had given you a hard stare, he had looked you in the eye over the top of the *goat-breath* tattoo and he had said to you, *yeah mate, I used to be a veggie too, but food's food innit?* Within a year he will be gone from this world, stabbed to death in a drug deal gone bad in a Bristol squat, the details of which are forever murky, but one version of which saying that he had hardly been nicked in the chest with a small knife and that his life had slowly ebbed away in the back of a prostitute's van parked in the street. Another version of the death of Pus goes that he had jumped through a first floor window, attempting to escape the drug dealers. Yet another goes that he was stabbed to death by five different people, most of whom will be dead themselves in a few short years. Nobody knows which, if any, version is the truth. But at the Wood Green Dole house Pus is still alive and he stares out at you through fluctuating gaps in the mass of sweating bodies, his head dropped onto one shoulder, his bloodshot eyes bulging in their sockets, giving you that same hard stare and looking for the provenance of the foamy home-brewed lager and the rotting yeast. Briefly your eyes lock and in the coming years you will often think to yourself late at night as you drift in and out of sleep, *I looked into his eyes, I looked into his eyes and then he died*, wondering where he was from and what his childhood might have been like, and knowing that there is nothing to it, there is nothing to it at all, that there is really nothing to anything, that everything is all just random coincidence. You are frightened by his hard and searching stare, your furious dancing slows a little, you suddenly feel like a fish out of water, your filthy stinking rotten yeasty homebrewed lager all gone, and you push yourself back into the throng in order to escape his stare and its possible consequences, and you trip and you fall and nobody attempts to stop you from going down, and soon you are on your back, the wind knocked out of you, raggedy baseball boots and unlaced German paratrooper boots flying all around your face. You stretch your arms up into the air, unable to wriggle around enough on the floor to get enough purchase to upright yourself alone, and a slender pair of arms grips your elbows and pulls you back up into the perpendicular. You look through the sweating mass for your rescuer, and you see a fit young punk woman, and she appears to wink at you, and so you lunge towards her through the throng and you begin to dance together, spinning around one another and through all the others, this sweating mass of heaving intoxicated imbecility, as Sean and Napoleon from *eat shit* scream in their stereo guttural roar that *life is hard at the edge of civilisation, life is pointless, fuck living, fuck forever*. You find yourself face to face with your rescuer and there is a moment, and so you lunge toward her with your mouth, but she turns away and then she is gone, back into the throng, away. You turn back around, lost in the noise now, looking for another body to swing around with, and you see that Sarah is standing there staring at you as if she has been standing there and staring at you the entire time, and you shrug your shoulders and she begins shouting at you, she seems to be crying but you cannot hear above all the noise what she is saying. You shout something back at her but she cannot hear what you are saying above all the noise either, and she begins shouting something back and just as she does this all of the noise suddenly stops and you see her scream, eyes closed, fists bunched at her sides, *Jane fucking Spice!* but you cannot remember who *Jane fucking Spice* is, and then she turns and she pushes herself out through the heaving mass, out through the back of the throng and the heaving mass that has stopped heaving now, that is getting its collective breath back, and you push yourself through it too and then you are both out and onto the landing, and she grabs your hand and she pulls you into the bogs.

Inside, Hop and Neil are sitting in the corner sniffing glue from freezer bags, their legs crossed as if at yoga, taking deep huffs and mumbling at one another. You go to say hello to them, to ask them whether *axegrinder* were any good, whether they played *hellstorm* or *war machine*, but Sarah still has ahold of your hand and she pulls you into a vacant cubicle with its door hanging off. Inside the vacant toilet cubicle it is rank, there is diarrhea all over the inside of the pan and all down the sides too, and you go to close the lid but the lid is not attached to the rest of the toilet and it comes away in your hands, and you get runny orange shit all over your hands, and you gingerly place the lid of the toilet onto the pan and then you wipe your hands down the sides of your jeans, and you turn around and you sit down very carefully on the toilet lid and you look up at Sarah. She begins to berate you about *fucking Jane Spice*, and you wonder whether *fucking Jane Spice* was the young fit punk woman from inside, whether *fucking Jane spice* is a description, a description of an action and not merely the random use of an expletive, whether *fucking Jane Spice* was the fit young punk woman who has helped you back into your feet, while you were attempting to dance to *eat shit*, while you were attempting to escape the steely and threatening gaze of Pus, but you do not think so because the name *Jane Spice*, even without the expletive, because the name *Jane Spice* seems distantly familiar to you, but you cannot quite put the name to a face in your mind, but you are quite sure that the fit young punk woman who has helped you back onto your feet in the throng, in the throng that was dancing so madly and celebrating the musical phenomenon, the chaotic and wonderful musical miracle that was *eat shit*, that the fit young punk woman who has helped you to your feet, who has helped you to escape the baseball boots and the unlaced German paratrooper boots, that this woman was not anybody that you had ever seen before. You catch yourself and you see that you are staring blankly at Sarah and that she is crying hysterically. You stand and you tell her that you are sorry, *I'm sorry Sarah* you say, almost crying yourself but not quite managing it, you never know what you are sorry for, you never know how to talk to people, you are always saying sorry to people but you are never quite sure why. You go to embrace Sarah, to hug her, and she pulls back and she leans against the cubicle door, against the askew toilet door hanging there like a warning against exit, *DANGER DO NOT EXIT*, like a warning against unsafe buildings. You remember a local band called *unsafe buildings* from when you were at school, they did only *stiff little fingers* covers, as opposed to *hard times*, who did only *clash* covers, and it feels like a very long time ago, much longer than three or four years, and you catch yourself again, and you see that Sarah is still crying, and that you have stopped, and you wonder if you ever started. Then she bashes her elbows loudly and repeatedly against the askew toilet cubicle door, she is screaming, she is gagging, she is wiping the tears from her eyes with the sleeves of her flowery dress, and you lean forward and you grab her chin, you grab her chin before she can say anything and you kiss her full on the lips and you hold her, you try to hug her, and she pushes you back into the cubicle and you fall back onto the filthy shitty toilet, the filthy shitty toilet lid clattering onto the floor, and then she wrenches the cubicle door back open, and she turns to you and says *Jane fucking Spice, meh*, before exiting the cubicle and you think, *who the hell is Jane fucking Spice*, and you almost remember, but then it's gone again, like so much information, like so much everything.

You stand and you rub more of the orange diarrhea down the front of your T-shirt and the sides of your jeans with your hands, and then you exit the cubicle too, and outside Hop and Neil are still sniffing glue as if at yoga, only now Hop is drooling profusely and he has his big bald head touching Neil's, as if in a conspiratorial whisper, as though they are planning something important. Neil seems not to notice this as he huffs away determinedly at his freezer bag, and you think of asking Neil for a whack on his bag but you don't want to disturb them, they seem to be very into what they are doing, very into their moment, wherever it is that they are, and you think that maybe this is all that there is, that maybe this all there ever will be, and you stroll past them and back into the main hall to find Sarah and to see who is going to be playing next.

When you get back in there the throng is heaving again and *concrete sox* are halfway through their set, but you don't like *concrete sox*, you have heard rumours that their van driver killed somebody in Holland, and that some of them are not vegan. Nottingham is a rough place, a horrible place, an awful place, and besides they are metal, they are part of the cancer that is eating anarchist punk from the inside out, that is destroying anarchist punk with all of its ethics and principles, and you think that maybe this is a little strange, that this scene that has been your whole world for three years, that this whole scene is one founded and maintained on rumour and hearsay. The multitudinous throng however, the multitudinous throng seem to know nothing of these rumours, of this slander, of these urban myths about the personal behavior of the individual members of *concrete sox*, and they are heaving away as *concrete sox* power through *eminent scum, bitter end, euthanasia*, all the crowd pleasers, and you circumvent the multitudinous throng, you walk around the back of the multitudinous throng and you find Sarah at the back of the hall, sitting down, cross legged as if at yoga, like Hop and Neil in the stinking nightmare bog, she is sitting with Pete and Mary and Steve and rolling an enormous joint, and you sit down with them and you smile at Sarah as if nothing has happened, and she smiles back at you, and you stroke her arm through her flowery dress and she smiles at you again, and you plant an enormous wet kiss on her lips, and as you pull back she winks at you and you think, ah well, who needs *concrete sox*, who needs metal?

Pete and Steve and Graham are talking about Mark Dooley but Mark Dooley is nowhere to be seen, and you ask Steve where Mark Dooley is and Steve says that he doesn't know where Mark Dooley is, that it's possible that he's gone back out to the off license if the off licence is still open, he has no idea of what time it is, and that he has no idea where Mark Dooley gets all of his money for his booze from, and you say something underhand to him about Mark Dooley's banker parents who live in Highworth, where Mark Dooley grew up. Highworth is a sleepy dormitory village for such people as bankers and hedge fund specialists and molecular biologists and the like, in Wiltshire, near Swindon, population unknown. Highworth is described as *the gateway to the Cotswolds*, and is notable for its Queen Anne style architecture and Georgian buildings dating back to the 18th Century. The centre of the old town is designated a conservation area, its most famous feature the parish church of St Michael, it was once larger than Swindon and it is twinned with Pontorson in Normandy. Steve smirks but he doesn't say anything. The joint has begun to do its rounds now, and Steve and Mary and Pete are talking about the situation in South Africa, you know very little about the situation in South Africa other than some bands sing about it occasionally and you are supposed to disapprove of it and it sounds pretty awful, pretty hellish, but it has nothing to do with animal rights and although it does have quite a bit to do with the nuclear arms race you don't know this as you haven't read any Chomsky yet. They are talking about the Sharpeville massacre and whether it will happen again, whether or not things are really coming to a head over there, whether there will be a bloody revolution, the kind of bloody revolution that *crass* warned you all about, that *crass* warned you all to strenuously avoid, but you are confused because you always get the name *Sharpeville* mixed up in your head with *Al Sharpton*, the American civil rights activist who is of course black, you saw him once on the television at the house of your parents, your father grimacing at the screen disgustedly, and South Africa is all about black and white, South Africa is very black and white, and you remember that Poppy Edmunds, Poppy Edmunds who drinks a little like you and Mark Dooley but who is not here today, that Poppy Edmunds' father is a white businessman in South Africa, and that when he visited her in Gloucestershire in 1984 during the miners' strike, he said to her in his adopted Afrikaans accent that it broke his heart, the way that his former country, *this England*, they way that *this England* was quite literally falling apart at the seams, just falling to pieces, with the unions and the rioting, and you remember how that always made you think of the sleeve for the *subhumans*, Wiltshire's finest, how that always made you think of the *subhumans'* first LP, *the day the country died.*

The enormous joint is still making its rounds, it hasn't quite reached you yet, and now Mary is talking about the American military submarine the Nathaniel Green that has run aground in the Irish sea, you remember it vaguely from the newspaper headlines that you were desperately attempting to memorise in the motorway service station on the way up here that now seems so long ago, from the newspaper headlines that you were attempting to memorise in case somebody caught you looking up at the covers of the soft porn magazines, in the WH Smith in the motorway service station. Mary is saying what if there's been a disaster, a proper disaster, a proper nuclear disaster, it was an American military submarine, surely it must have been an American nuclear military submarine, *what if there's been a disaster and they're just covering it up, what if it's no longer safe to drink tea* she is saying, *what if all of the lentils are infected, we could all be dying, we could all be dying right now* she says, and Steve smirks and he says in an offhand manner that he thinks that most of the lentils come from Canada and Turkey and India, *which are nowhere near the Irish sea*, he says smirking, and Mary is clearly not impressed, Mary is clearly very worried about her tea and her lentils. In about three weeks there will be the disaster at Chernobyl but you don't know this yet, none of you know this yet, it hasn't happened yet, and when it happens you will see Jools Holland making a joke about it on *the tube*, on the music programme *the tube* that is on *the tube* every Friday night, he will make a joke that goes something like, *why should you always wear Y-fronts in Russia?* Even though Chernobyl is not in Russia but in the Ukraine. *Why should you always wear Y-fronts in Russia? Because otherwise Chernobyl fallout!* And you don't laugh, you don't laugh, you had always known that something like that would happen, but you had thought that when it did then the whole world would stop, but the whole world doesn't stop, the whole world just staggers on, like you the whole world just staggers on.

The enormous joint reaches you, and it is near its end, and you take three enormous pulls on it to finish it off, inhaling deeply and keeping the smoke in your lungs for as long as you can manage, the hot smoke searing your throat and the taste of the resin coating your lips and your tongue. The world begins to spin around you, the dark hall, the stench of it all, the last crashing bars of *concrete sox* playing *no trust no faith* wrapping themselves around each other as the nausea, like the *heresy* song, *nausea nausea*, as the nausea overtakes you and you want to retch, you want to vomit, you want to vomit black bile, and some of it comes up, the black bile, the imagined black bile, a pukey belch again, but you swallow it back down and you take in a few lungfuls of the rancid air of the dark hall, the stench of it all. And Steve and Mary are again wondering aloud just where Mark Dooley has got to, and you pass the now-dead joint to Sarah but the burning head of it falls off, severed at the roach, the roach burnt through, and it falls onto her flowery dress and she nonchalantly flicks it onto the floor with her chewed down fingernails before it can burn through her flowery dress, and you theatrically stretch your arms out at your sides as you fall backward onto the floor, in a gesture of defeat, and of defiance, you fall backwards onto the floor and into oblivion.

There is no lucid dreaming this time either, you have merely passed out again, and when you come to *concrete sox* have finished but nobody has yet taken their place. You sense that somebody is about to because Sarah and Steve and Pete and Mary have all disappeared, and you can hear the rattle of a snare drum and the sound of somebody's bass guitar as they check that they are tuned up, tuned up and in time, and you can feel something very wet in your pants, something like piss and runny shit, perhaps even runny orange shit, and in your head you blame the amyl nitrate, the amyl nitrate and the pot, those damned drugs, and you get yourself upright and you walk out of the hall, loping like a cowboy, out towards the nightmare bogs and as you pass the stage area you look across and you see that it is indeed *heresy* who are tuning up and getting ready to play, *Heresy*, Nottingham's finest, not Wiltshire's finest but

Nottingham's finest, and you remember walking past somebody earlier, walking past somebody earlier as they were saying that *heresy* would be the headline act, that *heresy* would be the final act of the night, and you wonder just where the evening and the day and the night have got to.

When you reach the nightmare bogs Hop and Neil are still sitting on the floor sniffing glue as if at yoga, and Mark Dooley is with them too, Mark Dooley is standing and Mark Dooley has a freezer bag full of glue too, Mark Dooley who railed so hard against glue sniffers at the bacon factory squat gig of 1983, the former slaughterhouse, in Swindon in Wiltshire, the former Bowyers slaughterhouse where an incipient *chumbawamba* played, and where Mark Dooley all but gave a speech into a feedbacking microphone about the evils of glue sniffing, what industrial strength glue is used for, what the fumes of industrial strength glue will do to your brain as they settle and coalesce onto your little grey cells. And you kick open what doors there are of the nightmare bog cubicles, looking for bogroll or something, or anything, anything to clean yourself up with, to clean your sodden stinking arse up with, but of course there is nothing, just as you knew that there would be nothing, and you turn back to Hop and Neil and Mark Dooley with their freezer bags, and you see that Mark Dooley is singing out some of his favourite *conflict* songs, Hop and Neil looking up at him enraptured as he goes through *meat is murder, the serenade is dead, kings and punks,* and you see for the first time that Colin Jerwood is standing there too, all six feet whatever of him, and Mark Dooley hands Colin Jerwood his freezer bag, their previous animosity forgotten, and Colin Jerwood takes a few hearty whacks on Mark Dooley's freezer bag full of industrial strength glue, the fumes of the industrial strength glue settling and coalescing onto his little grey cells, and he hands the freezer bag back to Mark Dooley, and Mark Dooley mutters something about his bandaged wrist and *that fucking nurse* cutting away his bootlace bangles, and then he forgets about his bandaged wrist again, and together Mark Dooley and Colin Jerwood launch into a furious rendition of *berkshire cunt,* their roles confused; on the single, on the single *to a nation of animal lovers: liberate!* the single on which the song *berkshire cunt* appeared, Colin Jerwood and Steve Ignorant, Steve Ignorant from *crass,* on the single Colin Jerwood and Steve Ignorant from *crass* alternated, they alternated lines and they alternated verses, the music so fierce and so fast, but now Mark Dooley and Colin Jerwood are confused as to who should sing which line, confused as to when and where they should alternate, and it is turning into a bit of a mess and so they attempt to sing the entire thing together, and it is going along quite well until they reach the furious crescendo, the climax, the climax in the final verse, *heart beats faster eyes wide and staring, death comes whistling cold uncaring, slaughtered animals slaughtered squaddies, their wealth is built from murdered bodies*, and just as they both reach the line *slaughtered animals slaughtered squaddies* Colin Jerwood collapses into a coughing fit, almost vomiting, almost vomiting black bile, and Mark Dooley collapses into a fit of glue-crazed giggling, and when Colin Jerwood recovers he confesses to Mark Dooley that he never could reach that last line, that last line of that last verse, that he always gets out of breath at that point, *always*. Colin Jerwood giggling now too, as he confesses to Mark Dooley that it took him seven days to lay down the vocal track for the single, even with Steve Ignorant from *crass* alternating the lines with him. Then he clamps an enormous hand onto Mark Dooley's shoulder and he thanks him, *thanks man I enjoyed that* he says, and he leaves the nightmare bog and you wiggle your eyebrows at Mark Dooley who is standing there quite bemused, and then you leave the nightmare bog too.

When you get back into the hall the noise is intense and the multitudinous throng is intense too, it seems to have swelled threefold, fourfold, fivefold, and *heresy* are getting into their third number of the night, *belief* from *face up to it*, and the multitudinous throng that has swelled threefold or fourfold or fivefold stretches almost all of the way to the back of the hall, and you attempt to circumnavigate it, you push your way against one wall, over and along, you push away the arms that reach out from the multitudinous throng, the arms that are attempting to drag you into its mass, into its core, into its hardcore heart, like a plague of zombies they silently beseech you, scum stained and pockmarked arms outstretched, *come in, come in, it's ever so warm, can't you hear the thrash? this beautiful noise? don't you want to be one of us? you really don't want to miss this!* and you are stepping over and you are tripping over crashouts and passouts and burnouts and people just attempting to take a break from the music without actually wanting to miss any of the music, this furious thrashing and crashing symphony, this grindcore heaven, and you push away at the slimy wall as you pass over the crashouts and the passouts and the burnouts and the people just taking a break, just taking a break from the beautiful noise, and then you are at the back of the hall, there is a little more room there, a little air, not much but a little more than before, and you push yourself along the wall, throwing your head back and gulping down rancid air, along the wall toward the jagged broken frosted glass window where Mark Dooley almost gashed open his wrist taking a swing at Colin Jerwood for reasons unknown, for reasons that were only inside his head but which are now all forgotten, even by him, and as you are almost there *heresy* stop suddenly, and you turn your head to look, you crane your neck to see, you stand up on tippytoes to look over the onlookers closest to you, and over their heads you can just about make out the dyed black and blonde dreadlocks of *heresy*, the dyed black and blonde dreadlocks of the beautiful noise, and then, just as suddenly, they are off again, off again and into *acceptance*, and the multitudinous throng, momentarily frozen, springs back into life, heaving and screaming, screaming and thrashing, the crowd pushing back at you, and you elbow your way all along its edge, looking up again at the jaggedy spikes of the frosted glass window where Mark Dooley almost gashed open his wrist taking a swing at Colin Jerwood for reasons unknown, and just to right of it, standing against the wall, you see Steve, black dreads tufting out from his shiny black baseball cap, leaning against the wall, smiling, another enormous joint protruding obscenely from one corner of his mouth, his right eye closed against the smoke, even at a distance you can make out the crows feet around his eyes, the design on the baseball cap, a *crass* patch glued and sewn at a very slight angle onto the front, a Chinese symbol that nobody you know can ever quite tell you the exact meaning of, and written above it, *fuck*, and written below it, *authority*, and somehow this moment is crystal clear, and frozen in time, and digitally perfect at 200 megapixels or more, and perfectly illumined, and many years later as you attempt to sleep in the Salvation Army wet hostel on the Whitechapel road in east London, the winos cursing and screaming in their sleep, if it can be called sleep, you will remember this moment, it will come back to you again and again, repeating on a loop, this perfect snapshot of the way you once lived and the things you once believed. And standing to the right of Steve is Gogs, his John Lennon glasses misted over, he must have had a good time the night before, and on his left shoulder a small tape recorder, preserving for eternity this perfect moment, this perfect snapshot, of the way you once lived and the things you once believed. You push your way through the back of the crashing thrashing multitudinous throng, and you reach them, Steve and Gogs, and just as you reach them the noise stops again, this beautiful noise, and you lean into them, Steve and Gogs, you lean into them over the stilled noise, over the silent ringing din, and the raucous applause for this beautiful noise, for the beautiful noise of *acceptance*, and you yell at Steve, *alright!*, and he winks and he nods, the joint not quite moving at the corner of his mouth, some ash falling from it, and then you yell at Gogs, *where the fuck did you get to Gogs mate?*, because just at that moment, your cynicism is gone, your innate cynicism has been vapourised by the beautiful noise. You are all mates, you are all mates here, it's just like it was at the beginning, it is just like you imagined it would be at the beginning, at the beginning just over three years ago, but Gogs yells back at you *shut the fuck up Frank*, and he indicates the tape recorder at his shoulder and he says to you, sounding really pissed off now, *shut the fuck up*

Frank I'm going to have to edit this now, I'm going to have to edit this now and it won't sound natural it won't sound natural at all, and just as he does so *heresy* start up again, crashing and thrashing into *trapped in a scene*, that most perfect of songs, that most perfect of numbers, that most perfect of titles, John screaming, John   screaming, *break the images of sexual norms, send them crashing not to be reborn*, and you think of Membury services again, of the WH Smith in Membury motorway service station, such a long time ago now, and the soft porn that you were attempting to snatch a crafty glimpse at, in your loneliness, in your frustrated exhausted existential loneliness, and your hypocrisy, your calculated and artful and despicable hypocrisy, the hypocrisy that all of these bands that you love rail against, the hypocrisy that you yourself rail against, and you slide to the ground, not falling, your descent itself artful and calculated, and when you reach the ground you see that Sarah is there, rolling another enormous joint, and that Pete and Mary are there too, and Sarah sees you and she touches your arm, and you smile, and you smile over at Pete and Mary too, and the frustrated exhaustion, the existential loneliness, all of that dissipates too, and just as it does the song, the song *trapped in a scene* comes crashing to a close, it's a very short song, it is one minute and fifty three seconds in length, but there is no let up, there is no respite, and straightaway *Heresy* launch into *sick of stupidity,* John screaming at the top of his lungs,

moralism dogmatism preaching – sick of stupidity! and
Sarah passes you the joint and you take two, three,
you take two, three pulls on it, and you pass it on
to Mary who touches your fingers, who strokes at
your fingers as she lightly takes it from you, and
the pot fumes coalesce on your brain, on your
little grey cells, and you want to fall backwards,
but there is nowhere to fall back to here, not here,
not now, the baseball boots and the German
paratrooper boots of the furious thrashers kicking
at your ribs and your ears, and so instead you fall
sideways, you fall sideways into Sarah's lap, and
she puts an arm around your shoulders as the
night and the music and the beautiful noise
thunder onward, as the night and the music and
the beautiful noise thunder onward toward some
yet to be imagined inevitable conclusion.

But after four or five minutes of rest, after
four or five minutes of resting your head in
Sarah's lap, you begin to come round again, you
begin to recover from the pot fumes that have
coalesced onto your little grey cells, and just as
you do so *heresy* stop-and-start again, launching
now into a favourite, a favourite song of yours,
launching now into *flowers in concrete*, and you don't
want to miss it, you think of *flowers in the dustbin*,
you think of *god save the queen*, and you push
yourself upright, you force Sarah's right shoulder
down and you twist your right ankle around,
almost doing the splits, almost falling back down
again, but singing as you go, and screaming as you

go, screaming *constant changes all around us, do we just mirror the society that surrounds us,* and you throw yourself back into the multitudinous throng, pushing yourself through, through towards the front, the arms and the legs of the throng pushing you back and then forwards, sideways and then forwards, you're making good progress, and singing and screaming all the way as you go, on towards the front, singing and screaming all of the way along, *some laugh and leave their sinking ship,* almost at the front now, *part of an iceberg of ignorance – the visible tip,* almost there now, *like flowers in concrete, there's only so far we can reach,* almost there now, *do the best with what we've got,* almost there, *we can only grow and go so far,* almost there, *and don't fool yourself otherwise,* and then you are there. The song crashes to a halt but the multitudinous throng doesn't stop for a moment, not for a nanosecond, not for one iota, as *heresy* launch themselves into *believing a lie,* and then *into the grey,* and then *built up knocked down,* as the multitudinous throng goes on and on, the hardcore zombies who were beseeching you to join them before, come join us come join us, don't be afraid, now a mass of individuals, then the throng once more, their arms and their legs and their sweat recombining and decombining and wrapping its limbs around itself, its sweat around itself, as *heresy* power through *cornered rat, against the grain, make the connection,* and you are at one with the throng now, your arms and your legs theirs, their limbs yours, your sweat theirs, and then, as suddenly as each song had begun, as suddenly as your life had begun, *slapped into life and slowly gutted*, their whole set, their repertoire entire, it all crunches to a sudden close and they are over, *heresy* are over, the night and the music are over, the day is done, and a bright light comes on overhead, flickers out, comes on again, somehow brighter than before, and you look around and you see the sweating hyperventilating thrashing multitudinous throng in its abject reality, *naked lightbulbs shatter illusions*, you once read that somewhere, *naked lightbulbs shatter illusions*, and you see the multitudinous throng begin to disperse, and you realize that you are done too.

But not yet. Not yet. You push the few remaining stragglers aside, you push yourself forwards and into the stage area because you know in your heart that this band, that this *heresy*, you know in your heart that they are the band for you, that this band *heresy* means something, like *crass* once meant something, and you want to be a part of that, this unnameable something, you want so desperately to be a part of this something, and so you push yourself through the few remaining stragglers to the stage area where the band are packing up now, where this band *heresy* that might mean something are packing up now. You want to interview them, you want to interview them for your fanzine, for your fanzine as yet unnamed, your worthy successor to *smiling and dying* and *fully aware* and *sheepscene*, you are not sure of the questions, but you're sure that they will come, the adrenaline pumping, the enthusiasm coursing through your veins and into the little grey cells, the enthusiasm something unfelt for some months, perhaps for some years, and you approach the bass player, you know that his name is Kalv from other fanzine interviews, his bass half in its flight case, his black dreadlocks intermingling with the two guitar leads clenched between his teeth, the sweat coursing down his chest and his back. But an enormous roadie, a professional roadie, not a hanger-on, not another drunk, not another amateur fanzine writer, he comes between you, he must be six foot three and twenty stone, he comes between you and Kalv the bass player, and he puts a hand on your chest, and he nudges you backward, it's not a shove, it's not even a push, he's almost absentminded, he's partway through disassembling a mike stand, but it's enough, and you take two steps back, and you stand and you stare, the enthusiasm gone now, the adrenalin depleting, the epinephrine leaving your little grey cells, and you look at the floor, you see the beer stains, the crushed dogends, and all of a sudden their stench rushes up at you, and you smell the stink of the puke and the industrial strength glue from the nightmare bogs, and the shit in your pants, and you almost retch just standing there watching, and you turn and you make your way to the back of the hall, where Gogs and Steve and Sarah and Pete and Mary are standing there waiting, like they were by the van out front of your house in Swindon, sixteen hours ago, like they were in the car park of Membury service station fifteen hours ago, and you go and stand with them. It is over. It is over.

Outside, outside, outside by the van, everyone there, even Mark Dooley with his gashed hand and his gluey breath, even Hop and Neil looking so strange in the glare of the sodium streetlamps, looking so strange not sitting cross legged, not now as if at yoga, their freezer bags discarded, their faces quite pale, and you all pile into the back of the van and the van starts up after two or three tries, Steve cursing, Graham up front with him, Graham riding shotgun, Mary the Shrivenham princess, Shrivenham where they have a beagle hunt, Mary the Shrivenham princess crashed out in the back, her head in Pete's lap, she sleeps. Steve is wondering now whether the van will make it, whether you will all have to find some psycho squat to crash out in, some psycho squat full of drug-taking deviants, it's the name of a song, *rudimentary peni, couldn't stand dummy and maddy no more, so you had to go, so you had to go to the psycho squat*, but the van starts up on the third attempt, and then you are motoring, out of Redvers road, up past Wood Green tube station, and then left and along the Bounds Green road, all the way along the Bounds Green road and onto the north circular, and Graham is very drunk, Graham has been thrashing hard, he has been drinking cider all night and thrashing hard, he is stripped to the waist, his ribs sticking out, he is stripped to the waist but wearing his battered leather jacket, not very vegan, the battered leather jacket that his absentee father bought for him for his sixteenth birthday, on a random visit, and Graham is saying to Steve, *do you want me to drive? do you want me to drive Steve?* He is the other one among you who has a driving license, he got it last June, the lessons bought from the proceeds of his job at Plessey Semiconductors on the anonymous industrial estate at Cheney Manor, where *metal box* is, Plessey Semiconductors where the rumour is that the parent company is Thorn EMI, Thorn EMI who make guidance systems for cruise missiles, lightbulbs too, television sets too, but also the guidance systems for cruise missiles, and Graham is saying, *do you want me to drive? do you want me to drive Steve?* but Steve is saying to him, *you're drunk Graham, fuck off Graham you're drunk Graham*, and Steve is hunched over the steering wheel now, the speed wearing off him, the exhaustion and the fractiousness coming off him in waves, and in the back of the van all is silence, no-one looking at each other, a disconnected small multitude, alone in the darkness, and the streetlamps wash over you, they wash over you all, their shadows pulsating a four-four beat, Mary the Shrivenham princess asleep on Pete's lap, and Pete asleep too, asleep and snoring, snoring quite loudly, and you lean forward and see, at the side of Steve's temple, that a muscle is pulsing, that a muscle is twitching, twitching with the exhaustion, twitching with the absence of the amphetamine sulphate, the amphetamine sulphate that settled onto Steve's little grey cells, all gone now, all gone now, the day is over, but not for Steve, the long road ahead of him, the silence all around him, that roaring silence, apart from the snoring, which is getting on his nerves, which is making the muscle at his temple twitch faster and faster.

Steve makes short work of the north circular and then you are on the Chiswick roundabout, the M25 as yet incomplete, and then you are off the Chiswick roundabout and up onto the M4 motorway, you are almost on the home strait now, the long haul back to Swindon, and the landmarks rush by you, the office blocks, the Ark standing empty, *an example of poor feng shui*, and on past the junctions, one two three, Thumpers Wood, Norwood Green, the silence quite deafening, the sodium lights quite maddening, flickerty flick flickerty flick, in four-four time, junctions four five six, then the Jubilee river, Eton little common, then seven eight and nine, Maidenhead and Holyport, the associated golf clubs and country clubs, Bird Hills and Castle Royle, and Cookham Wood, the prison, home to Myra Hindley, and ten and eleven now coming towards you, Reading and Bracknell, and the engine is juddering, the whole van is shaking, clackety clack clackety clack, like a train on the track, and more golf clubs, more country clubs, Billingbear Park, Mill Ride, The Straight Mile, clackety clack clackety clack, and the smell of burning oil, as Reading approaches, and Steve looks down at the gearbox, and Graham does too, as if it might offer up an instant explanation for the clackety clack, and the smell of the burning oil, and as you pass Bracknell, the clackety clack suddenly stops and Steve looks relieved as the sky grows less dark, and you think that this is an omen, the sky growing less dark, the lightening dark, the darkening light, and the van moves ever onward and then, and then.

And then just as you are approaching the slip road for junction 12 of the M4 motorway, the engine cuts out completely. Just like that it stops, dead, and the van fills with an acrid black smoke. You are travelling at fifty five miles per hour, hardly any other vehicles in sight, in the lightening dark, in the darkening light, as you move silently west, toward Swindon, in the April of 1986. Steve hits the left indicator and pulls the van sharply over toward the slip road for junction 12 of the M4 motorway, almost missing it but not quite, and a small truck, its brakes screeching in the eerie early morning gloaming, veers all of the way around you, all of the way around the back of you and across the other two lanes, sounding its horn at length and accelerating as it passes, on toward Swindon and the west. Steve puts his foot onto the accelerator pedal as the motorway slip road becomes an incline, and it makes a little noise, barely perceptible even in the roaring silence of 3am or 4am and there is almost a burst of life from the engine, like anarchist punk itself the engine not quite springing back into life at its death throes, but this lasts for a fraction of a second and it only serves to fill the interior of the van with more of the acrid black smoke, your eyes watering now, your throat gasping, and the others now waking, Mary the Shrivenham princess coughing, Mary the Shrivenham princess gasping, Mary the Shrivenham princess saying, *Steve! Steve! What the fuck is going on, Steve?* and the others waking up too, the others waking and coughing and gasping, Steve pulling the van over onto the verge, the van juddering to a dead halt, half way up the slip road, of junction 12 of the M4 motorway, and Steve throwing the driver's side door open and jumping out into the air, to breathe, and Graham doing the same thing on the opposite side, on the side of the verge, they are out and breathing and onto the verge.

You are halfway across the back of the front seats, the others writhing and waking, twisting and turning and muttering away in their early morning confusion, and you look back over at them, their shadows half illumined by the early morning light, by the eerie Berkshire gloaming, by the darkening light, and you remember a time, clearing up after a gig, at the Broad Street Community Centre off Manchester road in Swindon, you and Steve sweeping up in the foyer, sweeping up the broken glass and the discarded and empty cider bottles, and Steve looking in through the doorway, into the main hall and into the bar, and seeing the drunk punks all crashed out and disheveled and ruined, and Steve turning to you and saying to you with a wry smirk, from beneath his ever-present shiny black baseball cap, with the Chinese symbol that nobody can ever quite tell you the meaning of, sewn on and glued on all askew, *fuck authority. Look at that Frank, it looks like one of those old oil paintings of hell doesn't it?* he says to you. And just as this memory is cascading its way through your ruined and disheveled consciousness, the grey zombies in the back, writhing and groaning and twisting and turning, *like one of those old oil paintings of hell*, the black acrid smoke filling the van, just as this happens Steve and Graham throw open the back doors of the van, and everyone, all of the grey ruined and disheveled zombies, *your friends,* they all clamber out and you follow on after them, into the eerie Berkshire gloaming and into the darkening light.

The sun is coming up now over Walk Copse and Hogmoor Copse and Bartholemew's Copse to the east, but there is no time to stand and watch the sunrise, there is no time to stand there and watch the sun coming up because this is not a hippie festival, this is real life, this is real life all dirty and stranded and hopeless and lost, and Steve arranges you all quite carefully around the back and the sides of the ruined van, and Steve goes to the front of the van, and he opens the door, and he releases the handbrake, and then he turns and he shouts into the eerie Berkshire gloaming, and into the darkening light, *push!* he yells, *fucking push now!* his voice cracking. And you all push as one, and the van begins to move, slowly at first, as Steve takes the steering wheel and guides it across, over to the right, hard right now, over to the right and back onto the tarmac, and it begins to move faster and on up the incline, on up the slip road, and you hear muscles straining and you hear knees popping, and you look around you to see whose knees are popping, whose muscles are straining, and you see Hop and Gogs, only three or four fingers touching the van, only three or four fingers apiece, and Graham runs past to the back of the van, he throws off his jacket, this gift from his father, his absentee father, and he throws his jacket up onto to the top of the van, this ruined van, bought for £120 for the quite unofficial Swindon and West Wiltshire branch of the Hunt Saboteurs Association, this ruined van that has never seen a single fox hunt, or a beagle hunt in Shrivenham, home of Mary the Shrivenham princess, and Graham puts his back into it, the van moving faster, on and up the slip road of junction 12 of the M4 motorway in the early morning light, in the eerie Berkshire gloaming, in the darkening light of a damp morning, in the west country hinterlands of the south of England in the April of 1986. And Graham's jacket skitters off the other side of the roof of the ruined van, and it tumbles onto the verge and it rolls, and it goes into a ditch, and still you all push on, those of you who are pushing, Hop and Gogs and Neil putting their backs into it now as the van gathers pace, and you look over your shoulder, you look back around you now as the van gathers pace, and you see Mary the Shrivenham princess standing in the middle of the slip road, away from the van, all her energy spent, and she's bent over double, her hands bracing her knees, gasping for breath. And just as you see her, just as you take this all in, and almost in slow motion, you see a red Ford Sierra coming up the slip road, at speed, not expecting to see anyone in the road, and it swerves its way around her, almost putting itself onto the opposite verge of the slip road of Junction 12 of the M4 motorway, in the eerie Berkshire gloaming, in the darkening light, but just in time it rights itself, and just as it passes Mary the Shrivenham princess it sounds its horn, and the sound of the horn seems to pitch her forwards, it pitches her forwards and onto her hands and her knees, and onto the tarmac, all of the wind knocked out of her, her palms grazed, and then she gets her breath back, and just as she is standing, just as she is putting together her grazed palms and wincing, she is screaming, she is screaming, *did you see him? did you see that fucking straight cunt?* screams Mary the Shrivenham princess. *Did you see that fucking straight cunt in his fucking Ford Sierra?* she screams. *Did you see what he fucking did? He almost fucking hit me Pete, he almost fucking killed me!* But the van is moving faster now, all of you workhorses, all of you Wiltshire packhorses hardly registering the shock of this attempted murder, putting your backs into it now, all of you desperate to reach the cusp of the incline, of the slip road of junction 12 of the M4 motorway, in the eerie morning gloaming, in the darkening light, pushing onward and onward, so that you can finally rest, and Mary is left standing, but you can smell her rage, you can smell her excitement, on up the incline, it drifts up the incline, her apoplexy, her affrontedness, at being almost ignored, for perhaps the first time in her life, and she catches her breath once more, and she jogs up the incline, all of the way past you, and reaches Steve at the front of the van, Steve still steering, Steve still clutching the steering wheel, and Mary the Shrivenham princess remonstrates with Steve, *did you see that fucking straight cunt Steve, did you see him? in his fucking Ford Sierra? he almost fucking killed me!* she screams, as he clutches the steering wheel, almost hopping at a jog now, and appearing not to hear her, his amphetamine come-down momentarily forgotten. And then you are there, around to the left at the top of the incline, at the top of the slip road of junction 12 of the M4 motorway, in the eerie early morning Berkshire gloaming, in the darkening light, in this lightening dark, all of you straining, and pushing the van fully around the corner and into the layby, and you rest, you rest, you rest. Finally, you rest.

And you all collapse into disparate heaps on the layby's rough surface, old bin liners and crisp packets and cider bottles and spent Durex scattered all around you, and Steve secures the handbrake, and he shuts the van's door, and he pulls himself upright, and he stands there grinning, and catching his breath, his shiny black baseball cap with the indecipherable Chinese symbol now slightly askew, and then he says, standing there grinning he says, *Graham, I think that you lost your jacket there mate.* And Graham, bare-chested and drenched now in hangover sweat, his ribs showing in the early morning light, the sweat running down his hairy back, Graham jogs back down the slip road of junction 12 of the M4 motorway and he retrieves his jacket, his leather jacket, the sixteenth birthday gift from his absentee father, and in no time at all he is back up there with you. *It's fucking ruined*, he says, clutching it forlornly, *my lovely leather. My lovely leather jacket is ruined. There was dog shit and cow shit and everything in that fucking bastard ditch.*

Not very vegan though Graham man says Hop, brightly.

And after a while, and after a silence, Steve clears his throat loudly, and hawks up some phlegm, and spits it out to one side, his shiny black baseball cap, *fuck authority*, his shiny black baseball cap scarcely moving as he does so, and he says, *well, what are we going to do now then?* Everyone is sitting around in the silence, Mary the Shrivenham princess now collapsed into a heap, almost sleeping again now, her head resting on Pete's left shoulder, the sound of the early spring morning, the sound of Berkshire birdsong now registering with all of you, and Graham says, *have you got AA cover or anything like that, Steve?* It seems like a perfectly ridiculous question, you are all of you penniless and unemployed anarchist punks, your only mode of transport a ruined brown Sherpa van bought for £120 from the proceeds of anarchist punk benefit gigs for the non-existent West Wiltshire branch of the Hunt Saboteurs Association, even though Steve often refers to it as *my car*, as he seems to be the only one who can drive it, as he organised most of the benefit gigs for the non-existent West Wiltshire branch of the Hunt Saboteurs Association, but Steve says, *I've got cover on my dad's AA membership yeah*, he says, and he reaches into the arse pocket of his shiny black drill jeans. And from a cloth hippie wallet, with an om sign emblazoned in red, from a cloth hippie wallet he pulls out a card, a membership card, for the *AA*, for the *Automobile Association*, in the name of John Simons. *But,* he says, *it's pretty useless unless we can find a telephone box.* You, Sarah and Pete seem to stand in unison, and you all wander out onto the road and you see a road sign at the top of the slip road, the slip road for junction 12 of the M4 motorway, and the road sign says, *Theale, 3 miles*. And without speaking, the three of you begin to walk.

Theale. A village, not too far from Reading, population less than 2000 souls. And the three of you together, you Sarah and Pete, you begin to walk. You begin to walk towards Theale, where in September 1643, soon after the first battle of Newbury, in the first full year of the English civil war, there was a skirmish here between Prince Rupert's Royalists and the Earl of Essex's Parliamentarians. Prince Rupert's Royalists attacking the Earl of Essex's Parliamentarians from the rear as they were returning to London, and up to 800 royal musketeers and 60 horses were killed, and they were buried in Dead Man's Lane, here in this Berkshire village of less than 2000 souls, now less than three miles distant, as together you walk down the road, towards Theale, where in 1802 the topographer James Baker chronicled the village, whilst passing en route from Reading to Newbury, and he described it as *inconsiderable*. Theale, *inconsiderable Theale*, where Dick Turpin was said to have hid in a secret room, in the Old Lamb Inn on the high street. And you walk on, only two and a half miles now, maybe even less, to see if there might be a telephone box by the side of this lonely deserted Berkshire road in the eerie early morning gloaming, in the darkening light, in the lightening dark, on the road to Theale. You walk on. Looking for a telephone box, looking for a telephone box to call the *AA*, to call the *Automobile Association*, to be rescued, to be rescued from your self-created plight, and in the years to come, sitting in a damp and dark church basement on the Holloway road in north London, on the great north road, on the A1, you will meet a woman named Victoria, a regal name, cavaliers and roundheads, and Victoria, who has lived in South Africa, Victoria will tell you a story about her first week in *AA*, in the other *AA*, Victoria will tell you a story about her first week in *AA*, and about how in her first week in *AA* a yellow van was parked outside her house every day for week, a yellow van emblazoned with the sign for *AA*, for the other *AA*, and about how she believed this to be a message from god.

But imbued now with a minor purpose, you begin to chat as you walk. This is what you do, you tell stories. You tell stories to pass the time and to break the silence and to keep yourselves sane. But first there is the silence, at first there is only the almighty silence of this Berkshire morning, and the eerie gloaming, and the darkening light, and the lightening dark, with only the birdsong, the lonely Berkshire birdsong, and to break it all up you ask Pete a question. You clear your throat, and you ask Pete if Mary, if Mary the Shrivenham princess is alright. And Pete begins talking, yawning and rubbing his eyes as he walks, clearing his throat too as he walks, and he says *yes, she's alright, she's just knackered, that's all, knackered and hungover like the rest of us.* You are referring to the incident with the car, the red Ford Sierra that passed her at speed, on the slip road of junction 12 of the M4 motorway, almost knocking her down, instead pitching her forward and onto her hands and knees, down onto the tarmac and onto her hands and knees. *She's always doing things like that,* Pete says, *she's always doing mad things like that, it's as if she thinks that nothing bad should ever happen to her. But it's funny,* he says, *it's strange, we never argue about those things, about the big things, about the stupid things that she does, about the stupid things that I do, about the near death experiences, we only ever argue about the little things. What little things Pete,* you ask him, *what little things do you argue about?* Grateful now for the conversation, for the conversation that is breaking up the silence of the early morning gloaming, of the early morning birdsong of the murder of crows that you felt was an omen, coming toward you, like some yet to be imagined inevitable conclusion, and the darkening light. *Stupid things,* Pete goes on, *really stupid things, really stupid things like whose turn it is to do the washing up, really stupid things like whose turn it is to put out the bins, or is the toilet seat up or down, really stupid things like that, just stupid things, not life-threatening things.* And you look across at Sarah, Sarah who is walking with her hands thrust deep into her jeans pockets, with her head down, and you see that she is smirking, she is smirking like Steve, because she knows what is coming next. And you turn back to

72

Pete, and you say *yeah I know mate*, you say *yeah I know mate, it's fucking mad isn't it?* and you tell him the story, the story of you and Sarah, the story of you and Sarah arguing like demons, like snarling mad dogs, like rabid dogs, you tell him the story of you and Sarah arguing like demons or like rabid dogs over fried onions and veggieburgers on a wet Saturday afternoon in the winter of 1985. It isn't much of a story, not really, but Steve had witnessed it, and Steve is always bringing it up because he thinks it hilarious. You must have been arguing about something else earlier, arguing in your heads about something unsaid, and Sarah is in the kitchen making you both veggieburgers for your lunch, for a treat, on a wet Saturday afternoon in the winter of 1985, and you are sitting on the couch in your sitting room, in Church Street, in Gorse Hill in Swindon, and Sarah pokes her head out around the kitchen door and she asks you whether or not you want fried onions on your veggieburger. And you say that you don't know and she asks you again, and then you smell burning, you both smell burning, the smell of the processed soya burning, and she disappears back into the kitchen, she flips over the burgers, the burning burgers, and she moves them around in the pan, smothering them in hot cheap thirty-nine pence a litre vegetable oil, so vegan, so cruelty-free, you can hear her working away at it, you can hear her moving the cruelty-free processed soya burgers around in the pan, smothering them in oil, and then she is back, her head around the kitchen door again, and she asks you once more whether you want fried onions on your veggieburger, she says *Frank, I'll ask you one more time, do you want fried onions on your veggieburger?* and again you say that you don't know, and she turns back again, she goes back into the kitchen, not wanting the processed soya veggieburgers to get burned again, to get burned on both sides, because nobody wants that, nobody would want a processed soya veggieburger that is burned on both sides. And she flattens the processed soya veggieburgers onto the pan, and she removes the pan from the heat, and again she puts her head around the side of the kitchen door, and again she asks you again, her eyes slightly bulging, and her voice slightly raised, again she asks you *Frank, do you want fried onions on your veggieburger?* And you shout back your response, half-standing from the sofa, *I don't fucking know Sarah, I don't fucking know whether I want fried onions on my fucking veggieburger!*, and she's into the room now, and she screams her rejoinder, a plastic spatula dripping with cheap vegetable oil in her hand, *Frank, do you want fried onions on your veggieburger?* And you face each other down, veins throbbing on foreheads, the saliva flying, eyes screwed tight shut, tears streaming down faces, and Steve is leaning forward, his head in his hands, tears streaming down his face too, but rocking with laughter, and Spike, and Spike who nobody likes but everyone pities, because of his constant battle with depression, Spike is sitting next to Steve, and pretending to read from a novel by Jean Genet, which is upside down.

And Steve is always bringing this up, because he finds it hilarious.

And Pete smiles, and Pete nods in agreement and in identification, and you all walk on, towards Theale. You all walk on towards Theale.

You walk on, the story having killed most of the distance, it is less than a mile now, it is less than a mile now to Theale. And in the early morning gloaming, in the darkening light, in the lightening dark, you see the outskirts of the village, population less than 2000 souls, and you look all around you for telephone boxes, but there are no telephone boxes, and you see the dimming sodium streetlamps of the village of Theale, you see one or two houses, which are cottages set back from the road, their windows unlit, their driveways silent, their gates firmly locked, in the early morning Berkshire gloaming, in the darkening light, in the lightening dark, and still there are no telephone boxes by the side of the road, and you come to a junction in the road, a crossroads, the first junction that you have seen since the slip road of junction 12 of the M4 motorway. And on the other side of the crossroads you see that there is a hotel, it is *the vineyard hotel*, which according to its sign is a five star hotel. And its foyer is lit, and inside you see clearly an old man in uniform, who is mopping the floor of *the vineyard hotel*. And excited now, you jog across the crossroads, three as one, and you reach the hotel, you walk up its short path, up to the foyer, and you reach its front door, which is all made of glass, and you try its front door, but its front door is locked. And you peer inside, shading your eyes out of habit from the early morning gloaming, from the darkening light, from the lightening dark, and the old man in the uniform who is mopping the floor of *the vineyard hotel*, he sees you, and he looks up from his work, but then he looks down again, and he continues with his work. And excited now, you all bang on the glass door together, three as one, making a noise, and calling out to him, *hey mister hey mister*, as if he hadn't seen you, as if he hadn't seen you and looked up from his work, *hey mister hey mister we need to use your phone!* but he carries on regardless, ignoring you still, and his movements become slightly twitchy, slightly nervous, and he finishes his work, he finishes mopping the floor of the foyer of *the vineyard hotel*, and he straightens his back, and as he does so he looks out at you forlornly, and he shakes his head sadly, and he gathers up his mop and his bucket, and he exits the foyer of *the vineyard hotel*, and as he does so he puts out the light.

And you walk back in the silence, three as one you walk back in silence, through all of the three miles to the slip road of junction 12 of the M4 motorway, the day dawning properly now, the birdsong in full swing, the murderous crows, which had seemed like an omen of some yet to be imagined inevitable conclusion, and the time passes quickly, and you cannot think why, because all seems hopeless, and all seems lost. And you reach the motorway bridge of junction 12 of the M4 motorway, and again, three as one, you all lean on the railing of the motorway bridge, and you look down on the early morning traffic, that is gathering pace now, that is getting more multitudinous now, as the morning warms up, this almost sunny morning in the April of 1986. Some cars going one way, some going the other, and trucks and vans too, all with somewhere to go, and the three of you stand there watching them, looking down on them, and the three of you stand there wondering, *what the hell do we do now?* Thinking of hitch-hiking in groups of two or three, all the way back to Swindon, in the county of Wiltshire, and thinking of the lies that you will have to tell to your lifts, as you make your way slowly, a few miles at a time, back to Swindon, so close and yet so far, thinking of the yarns that you will spin, and the freedom that this will bring you: *who me? what do I do? oh I'm not working, not at the moment, I'm a computer programmer, I'm a forklift driver, I design racecourses*, anything at all, because this life that you lead, it isn't anything that you're proud of, unless you are drunk, or on drugs, or otherwise asleep. And thinking and thinking of abandoning the van, the brown Sherpa van, bought for £120 from the proceeds of anarchist punk benefit gigs, for the non-existent West Wiltshire branch of the Hunt Saboteurs Association, of just leaving it there, at the top of the slip road, of junction 12 of the M4 motorway, of just leaving it there, of just flying away. Away. Away.

And breathing in deeply, and rubbing your eyes, and trying to relax but not fall asleep, you see at your feet a tattered newspaper, and quite absentmindedly you pick it up, and you flick through the pages of the tattered newspaper, its pages half stuck together with the early morning damp, with the early morning dew, with the dawning of another imperfect day, with the early morning eerie Berkshire gloaming, with the darkening light. It is the *Sunday Sport*, you've not heard of it before, and you look at the front, at the newspaper's headline, which reads: *DOUBLE-DECKER LONDON BUS FOUND ON THE MOON!!* And accompanying the headline is a black and white photograph of a double decker London bus, there on the moon, there it is, in the sea of tranquility. And you laugh out loud, and you go into a coughing fit, your eyes streaming, your nose running, your throat rasping, and Sarah looks across at you, she looks at you sideways, and she says to you, *what've you got there then love?* Love. Love. And you read out the headline, and you show her the picture, and you look into her eyes, as best you can, with your eyes still streaming, and your nose still running, and you say *they've found a double decker London bus on the moon Sarah, look Sarah, look. They've found a double decker London bus on the moon Sarah. Look, there it is, there it is in the sea of tranquility!* And she looks at the picture, and she squints at the picture, and she gets in quite close, she is studying the picture, and then she turns back to the motorway, looking down at the traffic, which is gathering pace, and looking at you sideways, she says beneath her breath, *I don't think that's real Frank, I don't think that's a real picture.* And you look at it again, but it's impossible to tell, through your still-streaming eyes, whether or not the picture is real. And you flick back through the pages, through the dew-dampened pages, in the eerie early morning Berkshire gloaming, in the darkening light, enamoured and excited now, enamoured and excited now by this new gift to literature, by this new gift to journalism, *the Sunday Sport*, that you've not heard of before. And you find a new picture, of a topless woman, a picture in full colour, of Linsey Dawn Mckenzie, with her enormous tits, and you are immediately enraptured, with the full colour picture, of this woman from Essex, her head thrown back laughing, her raven hair flying, her enormous tits thrust out at you, in this new gift to literature, in this new gift to journalism, *the Sunday Sport*. And wrecked with exhaustion you think that nothing matters, and you tear out the picture, looking sideways at Sarah, who looks down at the traffic, the early morning traffic, her eyes not quite blinking, not quite blinking at something, and you fold it up, this tattered piece of newspaper, this portrait of Linsey Dawn McKenzie with her enormous tits, with her pneumatic chest, and you put into the top pocket of your shiny black Belstaff motorcycle jacket. And you say to Sarah, not quite thinking, *I'm going to put this on the wall when we get home!* And Sarah says, again beneath her breath, *yeah, or the ceiling!* And later you will realise that this was the moment, the moment of moments, when it all fell apart between you. And in a matter of weeks she will be in India with Harry, who is your nominal friend, like all of these others here are your nominal friends, she will be in India with Harry, you will have only been together for three or four months but in a matter of weeks she will be India with Harry, for another three of four months; with Harry whose name is not even Harry, with Harry who is only called Harry because of the *sham 69* song that goes, *come on, come on, hurry up harry come on, we're going down the puuub!* with Harry whose name is Paul. In India. Gone. From this moment of moments, gone.

And you turn sideways To Pete, and you mention the newspaper, and the bus on the moon, and the enormous tits, the pneumatic tits, of Linsey Dawn KcKenzie, and you wave the newspaper, and you waggle the newspaper, this new gift to 20th Century literature, this new gift to 20th Century journalism, and you say, *look Pete, look, they've found a double decker London bus on the moon Pete,* but he pretends not to hear you, he is embarrassed for you. And he pushes himself back from the railing of the motorway bridge of junction 12 of the M4 motorway, and he straightens his back, like the old man in the uniform before him, with his mop and his bucket, in the foyer of *the vineyard hotel*, in Theale, and he rubs at the small of his back, and he flexes his thighs, and he rubs at the back of his neck, and he makes an announcement, quite a minor announcement, and he says something like, *I suppose that we ought to be getting back to the van now, young Frankie. I suppose that we ought to be getting back to the van to give them the good news. Mary will be worried.*

And three as one, in silence you walk, three as one, through the low rumble of the traffic, now drowning out the birdsong of the murderous crows, an omen of some yet to be imagined inevitable conclusion, in the lightening dark, in the darkening light. To the other side of the motorway bridge, the motorway bridge of junction 12 of the M4 motorway, in Berkshire, on a Sunday morning in the April of 1986. And when you arrive there you see a recovery vehicle, not the *AA*, not that *AA* or the other *AA* but the *RAC*, and Steve is standing there, he's talking to its driver, and he looks up as he sees you, and he stands there beaming, as if the recovery vehicle driver from the *RAC* had brought him a fresh wrap of amphetamines, and he says to you through his grin, *oh hello there you three, we were wondering where the fuck you had got to!*

Shortly after you had left on your long march through the eerie early morning gloaming, to Theale, to *the vineyard hotel*, to Theale, population less than 2000 souls, and all but one of them asleep in their beds, a yuppie had come up the slip road of Junction 12 of the M4 motorway, a yuppie in a BMW, and the yuppie had stopped, and the yuppie had a carphone, and you are not sure exactly how, and Steve seems unsure as to exactly how, but somehow the yuppie in the BMW, who had stopped against all the odds, somehow he had managed to put Steve and *his car*, Steve and the battered old brown Sherpa van, bought for £120 with the proceeds of anarchist punk benefit gigs for the non-existent West Wiltshire branch of the Hunt Saboteurs Association, onto his *RAC* membership, not the *AA*, not that *AA* or the other *AA*, but the *RAC*, somehow the yuppie with the BMW and the carphone had managed to put either Steve or the battered old brown Sherpa van onto his *RAC* membership, and then he had left.

The driver from the recovery vehicle manages to get the battered old brown Sherpa van started again. You three, you Sarah and Pete, you three as one, the others either asleep or half-asleep on the surface of the layby, you three move as one toward the back doors of the battered old brown Sherpa van, the others either asleep or half-asleep

82

on the surface of the layby, but stirring now and sensing escape, sensing rescue. But Steve motions to all of you to stay where you are, to stay exactly where you are just for the moment, and he says something to the driver of the recovery vehicle, and you cannot hear what he says, and the driver of the recovery vehicle whispers something into Steve's ear, and just as he does this the engine cuts out again, the engine cuts out again, the engine is dead. Quite dead.

And the driver of the recovery vehicle says something else to Steve, he says something else that you cannot hear, and he goes over to the recovery vehicle and he gets into the cab of the recovery vehicle, and he starts its engine, and your heart stops, your heart drops, it drops down into your belly, because it appears he is leaving you, that he is leaving you here, that he has done all he could but he is leaving you here, and it appears that you are stranded, that you are stranded here after all, at the stop of the slip road of junction 12 of the M4 motorway, here in Berkshire, in the early morning gloaming, in the darkening light, in the April of 1986.

But Steve approaches you, you three as one, the others waking now, down there on the tarmac of the layby, and Steve explains that the engine is fucked, *it's fucked he says, it's fucking dead.* This engine that you all worked so hard to buy, with the benefit gigs, with the anarchist punk benefit gigs for the non-existent West Wiltshire branch of the Hunt Saboteurs Association. But then he explains to you that the recovery vehicle will tow you back to Swindon, to Swindon in Wiltshire, this dead town, the town that you left the most beautiful city in the world for, for love, for love that was not love at all but only loneliness and emptiness and desperation and despair and crazy subcultural lunatic fringe politics, and Steve explains to you that he will ride in the front of the recovery vehicle with the driver of the recovery vehicle, from the *RAC*, and that Graham, who is now sober, will steer the wheel of the battered old brown Sherpa van with the dead engine, with the dead engine that is now *fucked, that is now fucking dead.* And Steve walks back to the front of the van, of the battered old brown van with the engine that is now *fucked, that is now fucking dead,* and he helps the driver of the recovery vehicle to hook up the towbar, and Graham who is now sober gets into the front of the battered old Brown Sherpa van, to steer. And the rest of you, you three as one and the others now waking, you all get into the back of the battered old brown Sherpa van with the engine *that is now fucked, that is now dead*, you all get into the back of the battered old brown Sherpa van, and then you are on your way. And you sleep. You sleep.

And an hour or two later you are back at the house, you are back at the house in Church Street, in Gorse hill, in Swindon, you are back at the house that you left the most beautiful city in the world for, in Wiltshire, in Wiltshire where you were born, in the fastest growing industrial town in western Europe, on a Sunday morning in the April of 1986, the sun now risen in the sky. You are back at the house, the others dropped off, at their houses and at Sunday morning bus stops, just you Sarah and Steve now, you are sitting on the sofa of the veggieburger-with-or-without-fried-onions debacle, of friedoniongate, you are sitting on the sofa and you are drinking tea. You are drinking tea with soya milk, the last of the soya milk, the last of the cheap and nasty Superdrug soya milk, Steve on the other sofa smoking another enormous joint to combat his amphetamine sulphate come-down, Steve smoking another enormous joint which he is not offering to you. And nobody is speaking, but you can feel the tension, you can feel Steve's come-down, his amphetamine come-down, the enormous joint notwithstanding, and you can feel your own come-down, from two weeks of drinking, since the home-brewed lager was ready, since the home-brewed lager was almost ready, your guts creaking and leaking, and then, just to break the silence, you ask Steve what he thinks will happen to *our van* now. That's what you say, you say *Steve, what do you think will happen to our van now then?* And Steve takes an enormous drag on the joint that he has just rolled, on the joint that he is not passing to you, his tea balanced precariously on his twitching right knee, because he is left-handed, because he is a southpaw, and he holds the smoke in, he holds the smoke in for the longest time, to get the best out of it, to get the best effect, and even as you are asking Steve this ridiculous question, even as you are asking Steve this ridiculous question in his ridiculous state, newly stoned, coming down like a brick, deprived of all sleep, coming down hard from the amphetamine sulphate that got him through the night; and you in your ridiculous state too, coming down off your bender, coming down like a brick, from the home-brewed lager that nobody else will dare to drink, from the home-brewed lager that nobody else will dare to touch, which is just how you like it, the shakes setting in now, which is just how you like it, hardly any food for most of those two weeks, which is just how you like it, even as you are asking Steve this ridiculous question in both of your ridiculous states, you are thinking, you are thinking, what was it that brought us all to this? All of us? To this life? To this right here right now life? What is it that has brought Steve to this right here right now life? With no hope? With no future? Is it because he is a southpaw? Is it because his parents are divorced? Was he bullied at school? No, that can't be right you think, because you know that he bullied Steve Morris at school. Steve Morris the amphetamine sulphate junkie who is not a vegan. Who is not even a vegetarian. As if that makes any sense. What is it that has brought you all to this? To this right here right now? With no hope? With no future? You have had conversations with Sarah, and you know that, like you, she had a very unhappy childhood. Her parents preferring her sister over her. Her sister the pretty one, her sister expected to do so well at everything, to get a husband, to provide them with grandchildren. His sister now a clubber in Ibiza, having graduated with full honours form the university of club 18-30 package holidays. And your childhood was the same, not the club 18-30 package holidays, but the miserable childhood, the misery that was always in you, your childhood was the same, or at least very similar, your parents preferring your brother over you, and you remember your mother saying, *oh, we've given up on him* and indicating you before walking away, to make a cup of tea, to check on the Sunday roast; you remember your father saying to his mates as you walk into the sitting room, *his* sitting room, not *your* sitting room, not *the* sitting room, but *his* sitting room, you remember your father saying to his mates, *well, here he is, the Smith family deliberate mistake.* The great British mistake. Like in the song. But you know that it's hopeless. This codarse philosophising. This mental mastication. Because this is just how it is. And this is all that there is.

And so, even as you are asking Steve this ridiculous question, in this ridiculous situation, in your ridiculous states, even as you are asking Steve this most ridiculous of questions, you are thinking all of this, perhaps for the first time, certainly not for the last time, but for the first time with clarity, with absolute clarity, even though it is hopeless, this codarse philosophising, with your burgeoning shakes, with Steve's amphetamine come-down running now at full force, and with Sarah in the kitchen, with the kitchen door ajar, just like before with the fried veggieburgers, just like before at *friedoniongate*, Sarah in the kitchen now, doing some washing up, or mopping the floor, like the old man in the foyer of *the vineyard hotel*, in Theale, population less than 2000 souls, all of them now waking, and going to church. Just to get away from you, Sarah is in the kitchen tending to the washing up, or something, or anything, anything to get away from you, and you and Steve almost facing each other down now, and Steve taking another enormous pull on the joint that he isn't passing to you, and holding it in, and holding the smoke in, to get the best out of it, to get the best effect, there is finally some clarity. There is finally some clarity.

He exhales the smoke at length, and with a soporific grin, and with a wry smirk, his brow furrowing, as if mulling something over, while he gets the best out of it, while he gets the full effect; and when the smoke has dissipated, into the sunlight streaming through the dirty window at your right, the window that is pockmarked with fake snow from last Christmas, where Steve had sprayed the festive message, *yuletide wastings*, and a smiley face, just as the smoke is finally dissipating, he says, *well Frankie, I think that I might get my dad to tow my car up to the scrapyard at Coopers, see what I can get for my car, and if there's enough then I think that I might take me a little trip to Morocco, it's supposed to be nice there in the spring.* And unable to help yourself, in your vertiginous state, the booze leaking out of you, the anger seeping out of you, in your tall tired wired state, just like in the song, you say, *it isn't your car though is it, Steve? It isn't your car. It's our van. It isn't a car, it's a van. And we all worked for that van. We all helped to organise the gigs that paid for that van, we all helped to put on the gigs, we all helped to design and to flypost the posters for those gigs, we all played at those gigs, we all helped to clean up the rubbish and the puke after those gigs, that van, that van Steve, not your car but our van, our van that we all helped to pay for, isn't your car at all! That van was supposed to be for hunt sabbing Steve! That van was supposed to be for the animals! For the animals!*

And Steve says, whilst taking another enormous pull on the joint that he is still not passing to you, Steve says, after exhaling the dissipating smoke at great length once again, Steve says, *I think you'll find that I did most of the work there young Frankie.*

And still unable to help yourself, your impotent rage running full force now, you say, *since when do you do all of the work Steve? I must say that I've never really noticed that. All that you do is you just sit around and get stoned.*

And Steve says, *I do plenty, I do plenty young Frankie, I think you'll find that I do plenty. I think that you'll find that I do a whole lot more than you do, a whole lot more than you'll ever do in fact.* And he takes a final enormous toke on the enormous joint, on the enormous joint that he is still not passing to you, and he crushes out the roach of the enormous joint into a large glass ashtray that is sitting on the sofa to his side, to his left side, he crushes out the roach of the enormous joint into the large glass ashtray with his left hand, Steve the southpaw, Steve with the divorced parents, what is it that has brought him to this, to this right here right now, and he holds the smoke in, for as long as he is able, to get the best out of it, to get the best effect, and he finally exhales the smoke, oh so languidly, and the smoke dissipates, into the sunlight that is streaming through the dirty window to your right, through the window that is pockmarked with fake snow from last Christmas, from the only Christmas that you ever spent here, that you spent here alone, where Steve had sprayed the festive message, *yuletide wastings*, and a smiley face, just as the smoke is finally dissipating, he smirks at you again, with that wry smirk, and he raises his eyebrows, like Eric Morecambe used to, in a mocking way, like Eric Morecambe who always voted Tory used to, but he doesn't say anything, and you are unable to help yourself.

You are unable to help yourself. The combination of the snub, from the snub of the stub of the joint that he just has just crushed out, in the ashtray to his left, Steve the southpaw, the combination of the snub, and the wry smirk, and the dripping condescension, and Eric Morecambe's raised eyebrows, Eric Morecambe who always voted Tory, and the perfectly timed line, that has cut you to the bone, in your frigid exhaustion, with your burgeoning shakes. That perfectly timed line, *a whole lot more than you'll ever do in fact*, that has cut you to the bone, in your frigid exhaustion, with all of this converging on you, in this perfect moment, this perfect storm, you are unable to help yourself, and you say, under your breath but clearly audible in the silence of the moment, this perfect moment, this perfect storm, you say, *yeah Steve, yeah you do. For yourself.*

And Steve is up, he is up and he is at you, in this perfect moment, in this perfect storm, the ashtray to his left spilling onto the carpet, its contents sliding across the shiny brown carpet, in this perfect moment, in this perfect storm, he is up and he is at you, tears streaming down his face, screaming at you, snot bubbling in his nostrils, he is screaming at you, *how dare you how dare you, I do plenty of things, I do plenty of things for other people!* and now he is on top of you, on the sofa by the window, by the dirty window where he had sprayed, only last Christmas, just three or four months ago, *yuletide wastings*, and a smiley face, and now he is screaming, *you're just like Poppy Frank, you're just like Poppy, but at least Poppy knows when to stop!* and he is on you, and you on your back now, and him punching at your face, punching once, punching twice, and then a third time, and now drawing blood, and Steve still screaming, *how dare you how dare you*, and you screaming now too, and screaming for Sarah, *help me Sarah help me Sarah! he's lost it Sarah! he's gone fucking mental! help me Sarah! help me Sarah!* but Sarah not coming, Sarah still in the kitchen, tending to the washing up, or mopping the floor, like the old man in the foyer of *the vineyard hotel*, in Theale, or anything, anything to get away from you; anything. Anything.

And Steve gets off you, his passion spent, he gets off you and he goes back to his sofa on the other side of the room, and with shaking hands he begins making a roll-up, but he doesn't say anything, he doesn't offer you a roll-up, a further snub, and the war isn't over, a line drawn across the room, an invisible line, a diagonal line in the shiny brown carpet, separating the two of you, and madly you think of Winston Churchill, and his speech, and his soundbite, from his *sinews of peace* address, in the March of 1946, at Westminster college, and of how he had said that *an iron curtain is descending, descending across Europe*, and you think of how Steve used to say that he was born on the day after the death of Winston Churchill, in the January of 1965, and about how Steve had said that *he was making way for a greater man*, and how you had always thought that was a very strange thing for a revolutionary anarchist to say. And you get up from your sofa, you move away from the window of the *yuletide wastings*, and you stagger into the kitchen, holding your nose, you are holding your nose and your mouth, you are wiping the blood from your nose and your mouth, which is really not that damaged, and you attempt to remonstrate with Sarah, and you tell her again, *he lost it Sarah! he went fucking mental! he hit me Sarah, he hit me! not just once, but two or three times!* But Sarah is looking away from you, Sarah is not saying anything, because she heard the whole thing, Sarah heard the entire thing, and instead of looking at you, instead of talking to you, Sarah is scrubbing at the draining board, like Paul Morley cleaning his oven when his father died, anything to get away from you, and finally she says, *it's none of my business Frank, just leave me out of it will you, it isn't any of my business.*

How dare you? That was it, how dare you. *How dare you.* On top of *a whole lot more than you'll ever do in fact*, there was *how dare you.* That throwback to school, to Jane Hobbs and Simon Chandler and Christopher Worgan, those rugby and hockey playing posh boys and girls from school, those posh boys and girls who felt so assured of their place in the world, who felt so assured that your place was not anywhere in that world, you were excluded from it, you were nothing, just nothing, *how dare you, how dare you. How dare you speak to me like that, you grubby little oik.*

Because nobody is for you. Everyone is against you.

You go back into the sitting room, your head bowed, your fists clenching and unclenching, tears in your eyes, your eyes watching your careful footsteps, your thighs trembling, the muscles exhausted, your own careful footsteps sliding across the shiny brown carpet, across the invisible and indivisible demarcation line, and you see that Steve has gone, he has gone to his room to sleep, but that he has left his packet of roll-ups behind, and not caring about anything, you sit down on the other sofa, a transgression against the unwritten rules, and you sit down onto *Steve's sofa*, like *Steve's car*, you sit down onto *Steve's sofa* and you pick up his packet of tobacco, Golden Virginia, which at school you used to call *Old Virgin*, and you pick up *his* tobacco, you peer inside the packet, you see that there is enough tobacco left for three or four roll ups, and with hands shaking you make yourself a roll up, *fuck authority*, the strands vibrating with your fingers, many of them falling to the floor, *fuck authority*, onto the shiny brown carpet, of the demarcation line, *fuck authority*, and you think back you think back, to *potatogate*. At the beginning of the year, for a while Sarah had been at her mother's house, her mother sick, her father unable to cope, her sister long gone, to Ibiza and beyond, so for a few weeks Sarah had been at her mother's house, looking after her mother, and Steve and you had been alone in the house. Alone in this house together. And all of your dole money had gone on alcohol. And all of Steve's dole money had gone on hashish and speed, and there was little money for food. And you had bought some potatoes, and you had thought about those potatoes all day alone in your room, and at the time that you had designated as your tea-time you had come downstairs and you had gone to cook those potatoes, because you did not cook together, in spite of your anarchist-communist tendencies you did not cook together, not you and Steve, and you had come down the stairs and you had gone to cook those potatoes, but the potatoes were gone. And you had asked Steve, you had asked Steve *very casually*, really quite *casually* you had asked Steve what had happened to those potatoes, where those potatoes had gone, and *also quite casually*, he had fixed you with his wry grin, with his condescending smirk, his shiny black baseball cap balanced on his head, *fuck authority*, the undecipherable Chinese characters that nobody had ever been able to explain to you, *fuck authority*, and he had said to you, still smirking, still grinning, *I don't know what had happened to them Frankie, I suppose that somebody must have eaten them.* But barely two weeks later Steve had bought some potatoes, and he had gone away to a gig in Leamington Spa, *chumbawamba*, and you had eaten those potatoes, and Steve, upon his return from Leamington Spa, and *chumbawamba*, he had looked for those potatoes, and he had found them missing, and he had confronted you, and had said to you, *Frank*, he had said to you, not *Frankie* but *Frank*, *Frank*, he had said to you, *I left three potatoes here three days ago, now where the fuck have they gone, where the fuck are they, what happened to them? what the fuck has happened to my potatoes?* Not *those potatoes*, but *my potatoes*, like *my car*, that unbelievable and *bizarre sense of entitlement*, a quarter of a century ahead of its time, before the phrase came in, before the buzz words came in, to be used against the poor, again and again, that *bizarre sense of entitlement*, and you had said to him, *well, I don't know Steve, I suppose that somebody must have eaten them*, and you had flashed him a wry grin of your own, and you had gone upstairs. And now, as you smoke his last but three roll up, now what is the word for that, penultimate removed to the power of three, you don't know, and now as you smoke his last but three roll up, only now do you wonder whether Steve had been acting, whether had Steve had been taking the piss. The ridiculousness of it all, *friedoniongate, potatogate*. But you do not think so. Somehow you do not think so. And you finish the roll up, and you smoke the roll up down as far as you are able, holding the smoke in to get the best out of it, to get the best effect, Sarah still in the kitchen, making small noises, what can she be doing now, anything to get away from you, and you finish the roll up, your fingers burning at the end of it, your yellowed and calloused fingers burning, and you toss its remains, you toss off your leavings, onto the brown shiny carpet, onto the invisible indivisible demarcation line, and you get up, you stand, your head spinning, your bowels moving now, but you not wanting to go to the bog, to the bathroom, which is through the kitchen, which would mean walking past Sarah in the kitchen, with her meaningless choring, with her silent clattering, and her *it's none of my business Frank, just leave me out of it will you, it isn't any of my business,* and you stand, your head spinning, your bowels churning, and you leave the sitting room, and you go up the stairs, you go up the stairs to sleep.

And as you sleep you dream. It is always like this, coming off a bender, you sleep a little at first, the exhaustion washing over you, the promise of peace lurching toward you at speed, but then ten minutes later you are awake again, drenched in sweat, the shakes racking your tortured remains, and you toss and you turn, in your foul stinking pit, and eventually sleep comes, but it is not an easy sleep, it is never an easy sleep. And there are dreams. Many years later, in the dank dark basements on the Holloway road, at the bottom of the A1, in north London, in the meetings of *AA*, not that *AA* but the other *AA*, you will hear these dreams referred to over and over again as *the horrors*. Because that is what they are. That is exactly what they are. These are not *dreams*, these are *the horrors*.

In the first dream you are lying in your bed, in the too-short bed, in your old room at the house of your parents, and then like now you are half awake half asleep, so that you do not know what is real and what is not real, and you dream of your mother in high heels, in purple stockings, she is coming out of your brother Phil's room, just across the too small landing, she is moving hurriedly across the too-small landing, to get away, in case she is seen, and that is all you can see, not her face, just the lower half of her legs, it might not even be her, but hurrying, hurrying, in the high heels and the purple stockings, but your mother never wore high heels, and your mother never wore purple stockings, that would be *slovenly*, that would be *common*, but you know what it means, you know what it means, this dream, this dream, you know what this dream means, and what this dream means is that your mother will always choose your brother Phil over you, always, and that is what has brought you from there to here, from a small in house in the most beautiful city in the world, to here, to a small house in Swindon, in Wiltshire, to you laying in a stinking pit of a bed in the fastest growing industrial town in western Europe, lost and alone, not a friend in the world, desperate and dying, of loneliness, and dying of alienation, and dying of exhaustion, and dying of the shakes and of maybe malnutrition, in a crazyass youth cult with crazyass rules, with crazyass unwritten rules, right here and right now, right here. Right now. In hell.

And you awake from *the horrors*, if only for a moment, and you toss and you turn, twisting in the filthy sheets, drenched in sweat, your teeth chattering, your guts wrenching, and then you are off again, and you dream again, you are back in *the horrors*, and you dream this time of a deserted Swindon, of Princes street, in the town centre, on a grey Sunday morning, and your brother is there, he is stripped to the waist, he is standing in the middle of the dual carriageway, wearing only his old school trousers, made of cheap polyester, the creases ironed in, wearing only cheap training shoes, not leather, from Marks & Spencer, even though he is not a vegan, as far as you know, and his face is all messed up and bloody, there is blood all the way down his hairless bare chest, there is blood on his cheap training shoes, and there is blood on the road, and you are standing in front of him, your fists bloodied too, your bloodied fists clenching and unclenching, you are standing in front of him, you are beating him to death, there on a grey cobalt-skied and overcast Sunday morning, in Swindon, in Wiltshire, in the fastest industrial town in western Europe. And in reality your brother is housebound, he barely speaks to your parents, because he has agoraphobia, although it is undiagnosed, because he will not go to see anybody about it, and your parents will not force him, because that wouldn't be right, that wouldn't be right. And in the years to come, this undiagnosed diagnosis will change, this undiagnosed diagnosis will change from agoraphobia to schizophrenia, but still there is no proper diagnosis, only speculative conversations between your parents and their doctor, and one or two scant visits, from a medical emissary from the DWP, in the days when they helped people, in the days when they actually tried to help people, but nobody is ever quite sure, what it is, what it is. Nobody is ever quite sure what it is. But you think that you know what it is. It is the alienation, it is the loneliness, it is the hopelessness, the exhaustion, it is the soul crunching bone crushing hopelessness, it is the living death. And in the years that will follow you will have many such dreams, and they are always the same. Sometimes they are a part and parcel of *the horrors*, but they will continue long after you have finally managed to stop drinking and drugging, long after several rehabs and even long after a plastic and manufactured *spiritual experience*. It is always the Sunday mornings. Like in the song. Johnny Cash or Kris Kristofferson or Sham 69, it is just like in the song. The alienation. The loneliness, the hopelessness, the exhaustion, the soul crunching bone crushing hopelessness, the living death. The living death.

Eventually you will sleep, you will actually sleep, but when you awake everything will be much the same. You will be drenched in sweat and shaking but everything will be much the same. There is only the darkness, and the darkening light. The world does not end simply because you are unable to live in it. The world goes on without you. Without you. Without you.